Complete Short Stories

Books by Ronald Firbank

NOVELS

Vainglory (1915)
Inclinations (1916)
Caprice (1917)
Valmouth (1919)
Santal (1921)
The Flower Beneath the Foot (1923)
Prancing Nigger (Sorrow in Sunlight *in U.K.*) (1924)
Concerning the Eccentricities of Cardinal Pirelli (1926)
The Artificial Princess (1934)
The New Rythum and Other Pieces (1962)

DRAMA

The Princess Zoubaroff (1920)

RONALD FIRBANK

Complete Short Stories

Edited by Steven Moore

Dalkey Archive Press

Library of Congress Cataloging in Publication Data
Firbank, Ronald, 1886-1926.
    [Short stories]
    Complete short stories / Ronald Firbank; edited by Steven Moore.
    I. Moore, Steven, 1951-   . II. Title.
PR6011.I7A6 1990   823'.912—dc20   90-33391
ISBN: 0-916583-60-0

First Edition

Partially funded by grants from The National Endowment for the Arts and
The Illinois Arts Council.

The Dalkey Archive Press
1817 North 79th Avenue
Elmwood Park, IL 60635 USA

*Printed on permanent/durable acid-free paper and bound in the United
States of America.*

Contents

True Love   3
When Widows Love   12
A Study in Temperament   21
La Princesse aux Soleils   30
Far Away   35
Odette d'Antrevernes   37
Harmonie   49
The Legend of Saint Gabrielle   52
Souvenir d'Automne   56
The Singing Bird & the Moon   58
Her Dearest Friend   66
The Wavering Disciple   74
A Study in Opal   85
A Tragedy in Green   104
Lady Appledore's Mésalliance   117

Appendix
    The Wind & the Roses   151
    An Early Flemish Painter   153
    Textual Notes   157

Complete Short Stories

True Love

I

He was very nervous. . . . Several times he got up and paced the room, but this only seemed to increase his agitation.

At last he sat down again and began examining the room as if he had never seen it before.

The walls were covered in old Italian leather of a pale dead gold, with here and there a touch of green. The parquet floor was strewn with Persian carpets, wonderfully designed, and so old that the colours seemed to melt into a faded harmony of red. Above the fireplace, and let into a panel of the wall, a XIV century Madonna surveyed the room with calm eyes; her long pale hands out turned in exaltation, and on her knee an infant Christ.

Against the pale gold leather wall a quantity of white camellias were banked up in old mahogany flower stands, between them and at even distances, stood suits of armour, which shone with a cold glitter in the dimly lighted room.

Half drawn across a great door—Gothic in shape—a heavy portière of purple brocade drooped mysteriously.

There was a profusion of brocade about the room thrown carelessly over things, and on a small ivory table, very high,

3

and wonderfully carved, a great silver crucifix stood surrounded by fresh violets.

At the far end of the room, on a raised dais stood a grand
piano half hidden in a pale green velvet cover fringed with
silver, and beside it a tall music stand, with a book of open
music.

Just beyond a sort of tent in purple and rose silk covered,
like an immense parasol, a large divan of cushions and skins.

The young man looked at the room as if he had never seen
it before.

Strange; for he had been there often. But he was going
away— perhaps though he was saying good-bye to the room
. . . . Outside he heard the bells of Notre Dame ringing; it
was a fête day, and now and again a cab would pass quickly
down the quiet street, and he listened attentively to the
sound as it died away, and was quickly swallowed up in the
noise of Paris. He felt dreadfully sad—he almost wanted to
cry!

He got up and looked at himself in a glass, and smiled a
little at his reflection. His long pale face was surrounded in
an aureole of wavy golden hair, and his big blue eyes and
bright red lips contrasted vividly with his pale complexion.
He looked aesthetic. He was well, but rather curiously
dressed, his waistcoat was of black and silver brocade.

For a long time he looked at his reflection in the glass, all
the while, drumming his fingers nervously on a long black
ebony table inlaid in ivory, with lilies and kneeling saints.

Then suddenly he caught sight of a copy of his own
poems. He picked the book up and admired the binding—
He had designed it himself— It was very strangely bound in
coffee coloured leather, embossed with peacocks and butterflies, on a background of musks and roses, he opened it at
the title page and read *A Book of Poppies* by Alwin St. Claire.

In spite of the English title the greater part of the poetry was written in Spanish and French. The book was dedicated "To Miranda."

The room was now almost dark, through the thick rose silk blinds, the last daylight shone as through a stained glass window. He put down the book for he could no longer see.

The room was hushed and still as a church. Far away a clock struck seven.

Alwin St. Claire walked to the window, pulled up the blind, and stepped out on to the balcony. A light mist veiled the houses on the other side of the street. The trees below stood motionless, not a leaf moved. The air was very hot, Alwin felt as if he were being stifled by an invisible curtain. There was no one to be seen on the pavement, there was no sound to be heard—everything was very still—it seemed as if all Paris awaited the coming storm.

Far away he caught sight of the Seine flushed red in the last angry rays of sunset, and the two grey towers of Notre Dame were now almost lost from sight, wrapped in a mantle of yellow mist.

In the Place de la Concorde the lamps were already lit . . .

He turned round suddenly with a start. Someone was standing behind him.

II

"Miranda!"

A beautiful woman in black was standing in the open window, over her left shoulder fell a great feather boa, and in her hands she held a quantity of blue and white violets. She was very thin and looked pale; her face was half hidden under the long lace veil that fell from her hat. On the front of her dark gown, was fastened a large diamond cross; she wore no other jewels. She looked Spanish.

"Alwin," she said, "tell me at once."

His voice trembled, and his eyes shone very bright.

"They tell me I must leave Paris," he said, "that I must go away and live quite quietly in the country—in the South— for a few years at least. They say it is my only chance."

She put out her hand towards the heavy tapestry curtain in the window to steady herself.

"Come in," she said, "and tell me all about it."

He followed her slowly into the drawing room now quite dark.

She went quickly over to the fireplace, touched a button, and suddenly the room was filled with a flood of rosy light.

Then she seated herself on a settee, and he sat on a crim- son cushion at her feet.

"Tell me," she said.

"There were three doctors," he began.

She breathed quickly. "Yes, yes."

"They examined me very carefully. . . . They say I have the beginning of consumption. . . . ."

For a long time they sat quite still without moving. A cab passed noisily down the street, then the voice of a woman selling papers, "La presse, dernière nouvelle la presse." The clock on the mantelpiece struck the half hour.

She got up gently without a word, crossed the room to where the great silver crucifix stood, half lost in shadow, and knelt down and prayed. . . . .

He watched her for some time, then with a stifled sob he buried his face in his hands.

She came to him, and kissed him on the mouth; she kissed his hands, his eyes, his hair. "Darling, darling," she said; she was crying too.

Outside the thunder had begun to rumble, through the half opened window the lightning whirled, the rain began to fall in great drops on the pavement, and on the motionless burnt leaves of the trees that lined the street.

Presently he ceased crying, her cool white hand on his burning forehead seemed to relieve him.

He began to tell her in a whisper. "They say I am to have no excitement, that I am not to write or do anything, they say that my brain is very weak— That I must have complete rest."

She listened looking straight in front of her. She felt too miserable to live—her married life was only durable, when there was Alwin to confide in—she could not bear her husband, her Mother had arranged the marriage, she had had nothing to do with it, her Mother was Spanish. And she, Miranda, was married to a Spaniard, an artist—how she detested him!

She had loved Alwin at first sight, she remembered vividly how she saw him for the first time. She was then a little Spanish girl—only ten years old—and she was on a visit with her Father and Mother to Alwin's Father, who lived in an old Elizabethan house on the seacoast in Yorkshire. She knew very little English having passed all her baby existence in Madrid and Seville, but Papa was English, and Mamma had always promised her that one day she should visit Papa's country. So here she was in England on a visit to Lord St. Claire, she, little Miranda! She remembered every detail of that first summer's evening at St. Claire Hall. Through the lattice window of her room all the sky was green, far away she could hear the sea breaking with a great thud on the big black rocks, and in the Park the elm trees threw their strange shadows over the long waving grass, all yellow and white with the buttercups and the daisies. In the garden below all the flowers seemed asleep, the tall white lilies, the mignonette, and the deep red carnations, and suddenly amongst the pale white roses, she saw a little golden head upturned towards her window, two great blue eyes that stared at her

big with awe, a little scarlet mouth that smiled. . . . She
thought it must be an angel, and she called to the maid who
was unpacking her box.

"That is Master Alwin," said the maid with a laugh.

And so little Miranda had loved him at first sight. Since
then her love had changed, she loved him differently now, it
was no longer the pure love of a little girl, for Alwin was now
her lover, but still at the bottom of her heart, she always
remembered Alwin with the baby Angel face amongst the
blowing roses, and sometimes in moments of passion she
felt ashamed. . . .

She looked at him now kneeling at her feet, and a great pity
for him and for her, blinded her eyes with tears. His golden
head lay upon her black gown, his eyes were shut, from time
to time a sob shook him—he seemed to be asleep— Would
he look like that when he was dead? She felt afraid.

"Alwin," she whispered.

He opened his eyes.

"I am coming with you too," she cried.

He seized her in his arms, it was he who was protecting
her now. "Miranda! Oh Miranda!"

She shivered a little.

"We will go to Seville," she said, "we will go. . . . We will
go tonight, why wait?"

She disengaged herself gently from his arms.

"Listen Chéri," she said taking him by the two hands, "I
am coming with you to nurse you, I am coming with you to
take care of you—to love you, and you will get well," she
said, the tears rolling slowly down her cheeks. "God will
make you well."

Far away a clock struck eight.

They listened side by side, each counting the strokes.

"Eight o'clock," she said, "there is an express at ten, wait
for me here, I am going to pack my bag, and write a line for

my husband, he is in the country until tomorrow, he will find my letter when he returns."

She left him quickly, and he stood alone in the great drawing room—alone with his thoughts. He knew that he was ruining her life, he knew that he was doomed, and then after he was dead what would become of her— He dared not think.

"But I *can't* give her up," he sobbed, "oh God you know I can't! I love her, I love her, I have always loved her; oh God, you take my life away from me, am I to die alone?"

He looked round the room wildly everything swam before his eyes, the flowers, the crucifix, the dim armour, and the pale Madonna all seemed suddenly to disappear, and he was in a garden. . . . .

Far away he could hear the sea breaking on the rocks, around him he heard the sleepy droning of the bees, and he on tiptoe peered through a branch of blowing roses, at a little girl at a lattice window. Behind her burnt two tall wax candles, and she, her baby face half hidden in her hands, peered eagerly at him, surrounded by a wreath of jasmine and blue clematis. About her window a troop of swallows flew, and he thought that they had fetched her from over the wide green sea to be his little playmate.

He cried softly now, a great pity for him and for her blinded his eyes with tears, but he felt almost happy, he felt purer and better for this struggle, this great sacrifice had ennobled him.

He looked beautiful as he stood under the great Gothic door, his white face outlined against the purple portière.

He took one last glance at the great silent room, suddenly his eyes fell on a bunch of blue and white violets which she had let fall on to the floor.

He ran forward, took them, and kissed them, "She and me," he whispered and slipped quietly out of the room.

❦

A few moments later, she entered the drawing room. She wore a simple black traveling gown, and her face was completely hidden by her thick lace veil.

"Alwin," she called.

She went quickly to the balcony and peered through the darkness, "Alwin, Alwin."

There was no reply.

She returned to the drawing room and looked about her in a dazed way.

"He has gone without me," she whispered, "he has left me here, oh, it was cruel of him, cruel of him." She sat down heavily on a chair and stared at the clock, "I am too late," she moaned, "and I shall never see him again."

She stifled for air. She tottered to the balcony flung open the window and stepped out. The storm had finished and the sky was covered with stars. A little wind rustled the leaves in the trees below, the pavement was still very wet. At the corner of the street a servant girl was talking to her lover. She stood watching them; she saw them as if they belonged to another world, as if she were watching them from some great distance.

She saw the man kiss the girl several times, and then move slowly on, his arm about her waist. She watched them disappear amidst the trees, staring after them a long time.

"By now," she said to herself, "he will have left Paris," and with frightened eyes, she imagined the great black train rushing through the night.

Then the tears fell slowly down her cheeks, she no longer felt angry with him for she understood.

"He loved me," she whispered, "he loved me best by going."

Slowly she returned to the great drawing room, she picked

up his book of poetry and kissed it. "God keep you, God keep you," she said. She began talking to the book as if it were to him. She laid her cheek against the cover, and repeated some of the poetry to herself. "It is all I have left, it is all that remains to me of him," and she kissed the book again and again.

Then slowly she got up, crossed the room to where the great silver crucifix stood, and all through the long, long night she prayed for him. . . . .

When Widows Love

Mrs. Fanley dropped the *Morning Post* and sank down in an armchair.

"Oh the cat! the cat!" she sobbed—then she got up and looked at herself in a glass.

She loved looking at herself in a crisis.

Mrs. Fanley had only twelve expressions, she wanted so much to have another. After she had calmed herself a little she picked up the *Morning Post* and read: "a marriage has been arranged between Lord Portmann and Lady Berkley widow of the late Lord Berkley."

"Oh! the wretch!" said Mrs. Fanley drying her eyes with a lace handkerchief. Then she sat down again and tried to collect her thoughts. She had been a widow now for eighteen months. She felt almost obsolete, it is so rare to be a widow after eighteen months, especially when one is a clever woman! "I should have been married six months ago," said Mrs. Fanley; trying to keep back her tears, "but it is so hard to find another husband with all these Americans about . . ." she sobbed. Then hearing the butler in the hall, she made an effort to calm herself, and began to arrange a bowl of roses.

She made pathetic noises in her throat, and pricked her fingers with the rose thorns. "Nothing shall induce me to go into mauve," she said: "I shall be quite brave and live only for my dressmaker and for my garden."

But she could think of nothing else but Lady Berkley. Who *was* Lady Berkley? she asked herself. Before her marriage she was simply no one; people had even said that her father was a dentist!

Mrs. Fanley shuddered.

Lady Berkley had been a Miss Vera Smith, until she had married Lord Berkley. And now she would be Lady Portmann . . . "The thief," moaned Mrs. Fanley, "she has stolen two peers!" She had felt so sure of Lord Portmann. And how much she had suffered for him! She had endured two whole cycles of the *Ring,* simply because she knew Lord Portmann was devoted to music, and was sure to be there. Covent Garden! Wagner! Mrs. Fanley closed her eyes. And then that terrible night after *The Walkuries,* what with the heat, and trying to appear enthusiastic, and the tortures of an eighteen inch waist she had fainted, and she almost blushed to think of the dreadful things she said of Wagner as she was coming to, and the horrified expression on Lord Portmann's face.

Lord Portmann had already been married *once* to an American who had left him all her fortune— There was something so second hand about it all— A young widower, and a young widow! Lord Portmann had lost his wife just at the same time as Lady Berkley had lost her husband; it was in consoling each other no doubt that they had become engaged.

And the tragedy of it all was that they were both coming to stay at Fanley Court for the weekend.

Mrs. Fanley was expecting quite a flock of friends from Saturday to Monday.

Her weekends were a noted success. She arranged a circle of deck chairs under the lime trees on her lawn, and everyone slept. It was so restful her friends said, and then when one could not sleep one could always talk scandal to one's neighbour, with one's eyes closed.

"Today is Tuesday," said Mrs. Fanley reflecting. "I have four days. Oh! if I could only drown her," she said furiously. She was looking delightful and her large brown hat went so well with her hair. Mrs. Fanley paused to admire herself. "Dear little widow," she said to her reflection. "We shall see," and she laughed.

❦

It was Saturday afternoon, and Mrs. Fanley watched her sleeping guests through half closed eyes. Lady Berkley dozed on a sofa next to Lord Portmann. "She is really in a most improper position," thought Mrs. Fanley; "and I am sure she is fatter than she was; I do hope so," she added charitably.

Lady Berkley was not asleep, she was spending Lord Portmann's money in imagination; she would have a house in Park Lane and a flat in Paris. And, she would make him buy all dear little Mrs. Hamilton's rubies when they were sold next month at Christies. She opened an eye, and looked at Lord Portmann. "I am sure he will rise . . ." she thought, and she began fanning herself with a small branch of leaves.

"Are you awake dearest Vera?" asked Mrs. Fanley who had been watching her.

Lady Berkley looked away from Lord Portmann; "Yes, Maude, and I have had such beautiful dreams."

"I am expecting the Vicar's wife," said Mrs. Fanley religiously, "she and her husband are coming for tea."

"Tea?" said a stout woman in a muslin dress, waking up— "I am starving."

"Not for another ten minutes, Lady Amberly," said Lord Portmann.

Lady Amberly groaned, and turning over went to sleep again.

"Just as if she were in bed!" whispered Lady Berkley.

"She is always hungry," said Lord Portmann, "she eats more than any woman in London . . ."

"How horrid of her," said someone sleepily.

"The Princess will roll off her chair," said Lord Portmann. Everyone looked.

"I am not sleeping," said the Princess, "I am killing flies!"

A shadow fell across the sunlit lawn, and the Vicar's wife appeared, followed by her tired-looking husband.

"How silly of Maude inviting her curates this afternoon," said Prince Borris to his sister.

But the Princess had caught an insect and took no notice of him.

"Where are we going to have tea?" asked Lady Berkley.

"In the rhododendrons," said Mrs. Fanley vaguely.

"Oh! but the wasps!" said Lady Amberly waking up.

"Dear Mrs. Fanley I feel I could not move," said a young girl who had been eating grass all the afternoon.

"Then we will stay where we are," smiled Mrs. Fanley. She was looking very beguiling in a large white straw hat trimmed with peaches, and she wore a large bunch of yellow butter-cups at her waist.

"At last," said Lady Amberly as the footmen and butler approached with the tea. "I have never felt more hungry in my life," she continued, "there is nothing like sleep to give one an appetite!" Lady Amberly was looking hot and patriotic in a red white and blue muslin, at the first sign of tea, she got up and straightened her hair, then sank down on her couch again and gazed hungrily at the peaches in Mrs. Fanley's hat.

Everyone began to wake up. Prince Borris moved over to Lady Berkley who was reading a French novel with a very illustrated cover, she put her book down, and became charming. Prince Borris was unmarried.

"Our Bazaar is next Thursday," said the Vicar to Mrs. Fanley.

"If you had *any* woollen clothes to spare . . ." said his wife.

"I am afraid I have not dear Mrs. Ayr, but I will see what I can find: let me give you some more tea."

"And they were seen in Paris," said Prince Borris to Lady Berkley; "of course she thought her husband in Scotland, and he thought she was at her mother's. The divorce is coming on next month."

"Poor sweet Clara!" murmured Lady Berkley.

The Vicar's wife looked shocked and gazed at her cup, but immediately looked away again for there was an improper painting in the saucer. She felt quite hot and uncomfortable; "I am afraid we must be going," she said to Mrs. Fanley.

"Good-bye then, dear Mrs. Ayr, and I will do my best to find some woollen gloves or something for the Bazaar. But won't wool be too hot for the working classes in July. . . ?"

"One can never wear too many clothes," said Mrs. Ayr, looking at Lady Berkley's transparent muslin.

"What sweet people," said Mrs. Van Cotton; a stout little American dressed in yellow and gold. She reminded one vaguely of a restaurant ceiling. She had her portrait in the Academy, which was mistaken by the public for a sunset. Everyone was sympathising with her for her only daughter had become an opera singer, and sang *Aïda* at Covent Garden. "I have been quite prostrate ever since," she told everyone . . .

Mrs. Fanley looked bored; things were not going as she had hoped. "I want to show you my new boat," she said to Lord Portmann, "we might go on the river for half an hour before dinner: who is coming with us?" she asked generally.

"It is quite too hot," said Lady Amberly, "and besides, dear, I am going to help myself to some more tea."

Lady Berkley and Prince Borris were talking scandal lying on their backs, and looking up through the trees. The Princess was catching flies, and listening to Mrs. Van Cotton, who was as usual talking about her daughter, she had come to England simply to marry her, "and now," said Mrs. Van Cotton tragically, "I am afraid she will marry a tenor."

The young girl in white was busily eating grass . . .

"My dear child," said Mrs. Fanley; "if you eat any more of my lawn you will die."

"Oh! I love grass! dear Mrs. Fanley; it is so restful and country-like after the London dust."

"Comme vous voudrez," said Mrs. Fanley opening her sunshade.

Lord Portmann got up, and looked at Lady Berkley but she was talking to the Prince.

"Are you coming Ned?" said Mrs. Fanley.

They sauntered slowly towards the river shining in the evening sunlight.

"It isn't yet six o'clock," said Mrs. Fanley; "we can row about for an hour."

She got into the boat, and he rowed out on the river.

"I have not half congratulated you," she said after a pause.

Lord Portmann looked embarrassed.

"When are you to be married?" she asked.

"November I think."

"Ah! so soon . . ." Mrs. Fanley was looking bewitching under her large shady hat, and big lace sunshade. She fixed her eyes on a patch of yellow water-lilies and seemed to be half asleep.

Lord Portmann began to feel uncomfortable, after all he had nearly been engaged to Maude Fanley and now . . .

Mrs. Fanley laughed suddenly. "Silly boy," she said.

"My dear Maude?"

"You can have your teeth stopped for nothing!" she

laughed.

"I do not understand you," said Lord Portmann.

"Your future father-in-law is a dentist," said Mrs. Fanley sweetly.

Lord Portmann bit his lip; "I must say," he began angrily, "I think it bad form . . ."

"My dear child," she interrupted, "you forget I have known you for five years!"

"A lifetime," he said ironically. "I proposed to you before you married Fanley," he continued after a pause, "and you refused me."

"I was romantic as a girl!" sighed Mrs. Fanley.

"You would never have married me . . ." he went on; "and so . . ."

Mrs. Fanley felt annoyed; really Ned Portmann was too dense. Ever since her husband's death she had done everything she could to induce him to propose. With an effort, she raised a tear.

Lord Portmann flung himself at her feet nearly capsizing the boat. "Dearest Maude, I have loved you always," he said.

⁊

Lady Berkley and Prince Borris strolled through the rose garden, whilst Lady Berkley made the Prince pick her all the most prickly flowers she could find. "I must go and dress for dinner," she said at last.

"Oh! another quarter of an hour," he begged.

They sat down on a grass bank, and Lady Berkley began pulling her roses to pieces, she was thinking deeply.

"When do you go back to Poland?" she asked the Prince.

"That depends . . . perhaps November."

"Ah! so, you will not be in London for my wedding," said Lady Berkley regretfully; then after a pause, "What a beautiful country Poland must be . . . It has always been my wish to go there . . . to live there . . ."

The Prince looked at her and understood; "we will see dear Madame, if it cannot be arranged," he said.

℘

"I want to speak to you, Ned," said Lady Berkley to Lord Portmann after dinner.

Lord Portmann had been talking to Mrs. Fanley who was looking charming in silver and white.

"I want you to take me round the garden," she said to him, as soon as they were alone, "I have something to say to you."

Lord Portmann followed her, and she began at once; "I feel sure we have made a mistake, I want you to understand Ned that I am not the serious woman that you think me to be! I should die in trying to interest myself in English politics. I want you to be charming and let me off." She spoke quickly and nervously, looking straight in front of her, so she was spared the look of delight that came over Lord Portmann's face.

"My dear Vera, of course, you surprise me very much," he said; "but if it is your wish . . ."

"I was sure, you would be charming," she said, "and now I am going in to sing the duet from *Samson et Dalila* with the Prince."

℘

"We are all waiting for you," said Mrs. Fanley to Lady Berkley as she entered the music room.

"I am so sorry, darling," said Lady Berkley, "where is the Prince?"

"He is looking for the music, we are going to sing something that the Princess has composed. Lady Amberly plays the flute," said Mrs. Fanley, "perhaps she will begin."

"So soon after dinner, dear, I would rather not," said Lady Amberly; "Dear Mrs. Fanley I must congratulate you, though," she went on, "your chef is an artist."

"We are going to begin," said Lady Berkley.

"Nothing from *Aïda* I hope," said Mrs. Van Cotton nervously.

"Ne vous inquiètez pas, chère Madame," said the Prince. Everyone began talking at once.

"No, no, nothing classic," said the pale-faced girl, "something from *The Cingalee*."

Mrs. Fanley manoeuvered Lord Portmann into a corner. "Well?" she asked.

"I am free," he said.

Mrs. Fanley blushed, a feat for a widow.

"Will you marry me, Maude," whispered Lord Portmann.

"I will reflect," she said, then, repenting of her cruelty, she relented. "Yes," she said graciously, "if we are married at St. George's, Hanover Square. I should never feel married anywhere else."

"Darling," he said, "I love you, and you are wearing a most charming frock."

Mrs. Fanley looked pleased. "I shall have a lovely trousseau, and we will spend our honeymoon in Paris, it will be quiet and restful for us after this dreadful London season . . ."

Lord Portmann brightened. "Yes, Paris!" he said.

Lady Berkley had evidently arranged her own affairs for she was looking radiant.

"I do not feel in the least jealous though," said Mrs. Fanley to herself, "the Prince is foreign, and perhaps," she added, "he may not be a Prince at all, one never knows!"

A Study in Temperament

Lady Agnes Charters leaned back in a Louis XIV chair and critically glanced at herself reflected in a tall mirror. Certainly the delicate green brocade of the *grande siècle* made a foil for her crown of golden hair which her women friends charitably attributed to Art. She was wearing black that day —a long, clinging gown that coiled about her like a dusky snake; her white hands, covered in jewels, shone like glow-worms in the twilight.

"There is no one like Lucile for black," thought she, "I am a symphony of black, green, and gold." Lady Agnes remained looking at her reflection through half-closed eyes. "If I could only persuade Guy to give me those emeralds, how lovely they would look in my hair!" She was noted for having the most beautiful hair in London. It is so nice to be noted for something!

Lady Agnes was always at home Fridays; she hated it, but then, as she said to her friend, Lord Sevenoaks, she felt so free when it was all over; so this particular afternoon, Lady Agnes chose a becoming and shady corner in her boudoir, and waited.

She was expecting a poetess, her sister-in-law, and, perhaps, her husband. She so seldom saw him, but then there is something so very early Victorian in seeing one's husband, except, of course, sometimes at meals.

Lady Agnes yawned.

"How very dull life is," she said to herself. "I haven't seen Sevenoaks for a whole week."

A bell rang.

"I hope it isn't my sister-in-law," thought Lady Agnes.

She looked at herself in the glass, and ran her hand lightly over her hair.

"I think I shall dye my hair *very* gradually to red," she said, "I am so tired of gold; of course those yellow tea roses match beautifully, but I think that yellow is becoming monotonous." She got up and went to a little table covered with books, and picked up a small volume bound in grey. "A touch of grey will improve my dress," she thought as she seated herself in the shady corner again.

Someone was coming upstairs. Lady Agnes opened the book, and found it was one of Maeterlinck's plays.

She hoped it was the poetess. It is so delightful to be seen reading Maeterlinck! So decadent!

But it was only her sister-in-law.

"Mrs. and Miss Corba," said the butler, and disappeared.

"My dearest Agnes!" said Mrs. Corba.

"My darling Lettice!" said Lady Agnes.

"I have brought Lobelia," remarked Mrs. Corba, standing aside to show her daughter. "She is so longing to know Miss —— the new poetess."

"Miss Hester Q. Tail. She is an American."

"I am always a little nervous of Americans," said Mrs. Corba. "But Lobelia, of course, having literary tastes—"

"What have you been reading, Aunt Agnes?" asked Lobelia.

"A—A French Author," said Lady Agnes, vaguely. (How trying of Lobelia!)

"I should think," continued Lobelia, "that it was very bad

for one's eyes reading in the dark."

(One's relations!)

A gaunt figure loomed in the doorway, surmounted by a pair of glistening pince-nez.

"Miss Tail," announced the butler.

"How sweet of you, Miss Tail, to come. I have a kindred spirit longing to sit at your feet and become a disciple," said Lady Agnes.

"I am so pleased to meet you, Miss Tail," smiled Mrs. Corba. "This is my daughter Lobelia, and she would so love your autograph for her collection. We have both read your poems on 'The Unseen,' and Lobelia can quote long passages . . . about little Minnie finding her mother in Heaven."

"I shall be most happy in signing myself sincerely Hester Q. Tail," said the poetess, "and it gives me great pleasure, Miss Corba, to find one so appreciative of my work. In America there have been nineteen editions of *Minnie in Heaven*. In England, I am sorry to say, only two."

Then turning to Mrs. Corba.

"But tell me, *dear* Mrs. Corba, are you *the* Mrs. Corba?"

Mrs. Corba looked alarmed.

"I don't know what you can have heard . . .," she began.

"Oh! I hope I have said *nothing,*" said Miss Tail, "only you know one always reads about your dresses in *The Peacock*."

Mrs. Corba looked relieved.

"Ah!" she said, "I only wish that all literary people could be exterminated."

Miss Tail stiffened.

"I should not call the fashion column in *The Peacock literature,*" she remarked.

The dispute was ended by the arrival of Lord Sevenoaks.

"How are *you,* Agnes?" he asked.

"Very bored," she sighed.

"Who isn't?" said Lord Sevenoaks, sitting down beside her.

"Dearest Lettice," murmured Lady Agnes, "do show Miss Tail my fans: they are in the yellow drawing room."

"I hear you fainted at the Gordons' dance," Lord Seven-oaks said as soon as they were alone.

Lady Agnes smiled.

"I didn't *really* faint, only . . . well, the room was hot at supper, the table was smothered with red roses, I don't know which looked the redder, the women or the roses! and then . . . well, it is so nice to be different to everyone else, isn't it? so . . . well . . . oh! Guy, I am so *horribly* bored!"

"My dear Agnes, you want an object in life. Art alone isn't enough. Grub Street is so very grimy, and good works are out of date. But aren't there other objects? Isn't there *another* object? If you would only look for it, the search would not be long, and then—"

"You talk in parables," exclaimed Lady Agnes.

"Well, then, if you would only leave your husband and come away with me, we would go abroad and . . ."

"Don't, Guy; someone will hear you."

"You are so cautious, Agnes, I don't understand you; you say you love me, and yet—"

"I am not happy with my husband," said Lady Agnes, "but then so few women are—at least, in our set."

"Then you won't come?"

"I cannot, I daren't! Think of the scandal!"

"You should rather say think of the evening papers!"

"Goose!" laughed Lady Agnes. "But I shall see you Sunday at the Princess's, shan't I?"

Mrs. Corba, who had taken Miss Tail a small personally conducted tour through the five reception rooms, now returned.

"I so love clever people," she was saying, "and may I call you Hester?"

"Oh *do!*" said Miss Tail.

Lobelia fixed her eyes upon an Indian idol, that stood on the piano, surrounded with iris.

"Agnes is so aesthetic," ejculated her sister-in-law.

"I love idols," said Lord Sevenoaks, joining the conversation.

"Don't talk about idols," whispered Lady Agnes in a low voice, "or Miss Tail may try to make an epigram."

"The ideal idol," began Miss Tail, and paused.

"Yes?" asked Lobelia anxiously.

"Is made in Japan!" said Miss Tail.

Lobelia looked disappointed; she had hoped for something soulful.

"Do you take cream and sugar, Miss Tail?" asked Lady Agnes.

"A little milk," said Miss Tail dreamily.

"You are very musical, Miss Corba, I should say?" enquired the poetess, after having mesmerized a plate of bread and butter.

Lobelia looked very pleased.

"Oh no! I am not very musical," she replied modestly, "but mamma is."

"I always said I should have liked to marry Paderewski," said Mrs. Corba.

"And you married a captain in the Navy! How inconsistent!"

"Not so inconsistent as you think," remarked Lobelia. "Mamma always says that papa reminded her of Lohengrin, which is her favourite opera. So Paderewski being unavailable, mamma took Lohengrin!"

"And does he remind you of Lohengrin *now?*" asked Miss Tail.

"No, the ideal only lasted a fortnight. We spent our honeymoon yachting in the Mediterranean, and . . ."

"Mamma is not a good sailor," interposed Lobelia . . .

"This is unhappily an age of facts and realities," said Miss Tail. "There is no romance in modern life."

"I should have loved to have lived in the Bible period," said Lobelia, religiously. "How beautiful to have followed the Saints!" Lobelia was engaged to a clergyman.

"How very true—" replied Miss Tail; then, after a pause, "modern life is only remarkable for its want of profile, and lack of manners. To be smart is to be artificial. To be artificial is to be smart. There is not a man or woman in London society that dares to be him or herself. We are surrounded by invisible laws and conventions, we all sin, and cover our sins in chiffon and diamonds. The chiffon is quite transparent, everyone can see through it, still chiffon is a veil, and then the diamonds! We are all vulgar at heart, and if the diamonds glitter, what does it matter where they come from or how they are bought? To be artificial, and to be a little more improbable and impossible than one's neighbour is to be a perfect success!"

Lady Agnes looked shocked. She had not been looking at Miss Tail, but at her own reflection in a mirror.

This was of course the result of knowing such people! She regretted ever having asked Miss Tail; if she continued receiving her she would soon have a reputation of harbouring socialists, perhaps Nihilists—how dreadful!

Lobelia looked interested; as a future clergyman's wife she felt she ought to uphold Miss Tail. Still she didn't like the remark about profiles. Lobelia had no profile; she knew it, and did her best not to show hers. But it is almost impossible to go through life without showing one's profile—at dinner parties, for instance.

Agnes trailed over to Lord Sevenoaks. "I want to show you," she said, "a new picture that my husband has bought; it is in the white drawing room."

Lord Sevenoaks followed her.

"Who are the two ladies with Miss Tail?" he asked as soon as they were out of hearing.

"My sister-in-law and her daughter," replied Lady Agnes.

"*Which* is the mother?" asked Lord Sevenoaks.

"The younger-looking of the two. Lobelia, her daughter, always wears such morbid-looking hats, they make her look quite ten years older than she really is. Her mother always wears black—now she is losing her figure. She always pretends to be in mourning for someone, simply as an excuse for wearing black; she has been in black now for three seasons."

"In other words," said Lord Sevenoaks, "she has been losing her figure for three years."

Lady Agnes regretted now having left her guests. Guy was so impulsive. She felt a little afraid. She chattered on and on, and at last ceased.

"Where is the picture?" asked Lord Sevenoaks.

Lady Agnes laughed a little nervously.

"This is it," she said.

It was a mystical Madonna. A woman, with a long pale face, leaning out of the clouds, the sins and sorrows of the whole world gathered in the wearied eyelids and the red-gold of her hair. They were both silent. The last grey light of the London twilight fell on the picture, and the pale face of the Madonna seemed drawn in pain.

"How beautiful her eyes are, they are full of pity," said Lord Sevenoaks. "She is alive, see how her lips are parted, one can almost hear her breathe!"

"Don't look at her any more or I shall be jealous," cried Lady Agnes.

"Don't, Agnes!" said Lord Sevenoaks. "It hurts me to hear you talk like that!"

Lady Agnes laughed a little bitterly.

"I hate sentiment," she said.

The room grew darker and darker, and the Madonna's face looked like a ghost from the white brocaded wall. The room smelt vaguely of lilies.

Lord Sevenoaks looked from the painted face of the Madonna to the painted face of Lady Agnes.

"Come," exclaimed Lady Agnes a little brusquely, "we are getting morbid. Let us go back to the others."

"Not yet!" said Lord Sevenoaks.

"Not yet?" asked Lady Agnes.

"No, Agnes, listen to me. You are not happy here, you have told me so—then let us be brave—and—and defy the evening papers! Let us go away; there will be a scandal at first, but what of that? There will soon be another to take its place."

Lady Agnes laughed nervously.

"I will tell you, Sunday," she said, and went quickly back to her guests in the yellow drawing room.

❦

Lord Sevenoaks remained behind a few minutes after Lady Agnes had left. How strange women are, thought he. "I believe if Agnes leaves her husband—but oh! she doesn't seem able to *feel,* she has read so much, seen so much, that she has lost *herself,* she has become cold, artificial, and almost cruel, yet with such a husband as hers!" Lord Sevenoaks started.

"Come, old man," he said to himself, "you are becoming sentimental." And yet, thought he, I remember Agnes when quite a wee mite! And he sat staring into the fire dreaming. The Madonna looked down on him from the wall, and her eyes seemed dim with tears!

❦

That night as her maid brushed her hair, Lady Agnes's thoughts seemed troubled.

"Shall I bolt?" she asked herself.

She looked critically at herself in a long mirror.

Then she said to her maid: "I may go down to Brighton next Sunday, I want you to have my things ready in case I go."

She looked at herself in the glass again and began dreaming.

"I am very beautiful," she thought, "but I think it would be an improvement to dye my hair red—very gradually, of course—I should so hate anyone to notice—"

Her maid closed the door quietly, and left her for the night.

The half-hour struck—the three-quarters—Lady Agnes rose.

"Yes, I shall certainly dye my hair red," she said.

La Princesse aux Soleils
Romance Parlée

Écoutez, Beaux Seigneurs et Belles Dames, l'histoire triste de la Princesse aux Soleils.

L'Empereur de Perse avait donné sa fille, la Princesse aux Soleils, comme otage au Roi des Iles d'Or; ainsi se terminèrent de longues guerres.

Mais la princesse n'aimait pas le Roi des Iles d'Or; elle aimait un jeune prince de son pays.

Un jeune homme plus pâle que la nouvelle lune, un jeune homme qui portait une cuirasse de bronze rouge parsemée de perles blanches. . . .

Tous les soirs, quand les grands cyprès projetaient leurs ombres violettes sur la terrasse de marbre rose, la petite princesse captive sortait accompagnée par ses esclaves noirs pour regarder le soleil couchant sur la mer.

Elle portait une robe couleur de toutes les fleurs, semée de perles blanches qui, quand elle marchait faisaient un petit bruit délicieux comme de la musique lointaine. . . .

Dans sa chevelure plus noire que la nuit, deux grands lys rouges brillaient comme des vers luisants, et aussi tombait de sa tête un voile couleur de la mer, qui flottait derrière elle comme un nuage bleu dans le vent du soir.

Dans une de ses petites mains blanches, elle portait un éventail de plumes noires; et dans l'autre un immense soleil, avec lequel de temps en temps elle chassait un papillon rouge ou un oiseau aux ailes d'or.

Les esclaves la suivaient en chantant doucement. Elles portaient chacune une lyre d'ivoire incrustée d'émeraudes et de perles; leurs mains noires semblaient comme des ombres sur les cordes d'argent.

Elles regardaient tristement de leurs grands yeux mélancoliques le soleil couchant sur la mer. Elles avaient la nostalgie du pays.

Leurs pieds étaient attachés par des chaines d'argent.

Dans les arbres les rossignols chantaient divinement, et sous les grands cyprès noirs les roses rouges semblaient dormir.

L'air était alourdi par le parfum des orangiers et au fond du jardin dans un bois de grenadiers se jouaient avec un frais murmure les cascades d'une fontaine mauresque.

La petite princesse marchait lentement sur la terrasse, suivie par ses Nubiennes; les ombres tombaient par derrière comme des fantômes sombres.

De chaque côté de la terrasse les soleils immenses et immobiles semblaient comme des soldats en garde.

A l'horizon une voile rose et lilas avait l'air d'un papillon perdu. . . .

La petite princesse regardait tristement le soleil disparaître dans la mer—elle aussi, elle avait la nostalgie du pays. . . .

Elle soupirait aprés son pays—aprés la Perse, et les nuits brûlantes ou l'air coloré de pourpre, parfumé de la senteur des roses la faisait défaillir—aprés le doux roucoulement des colombes parmi les orangers, et ses paons bleus qui marchaient lentement sous les myrtes, sur les tapis de soie blanche et rose.

Et parfois, parfois lui apparaissait son fiancé le Prince à l'armure écarlate, bruissante, tout couvert du cliquetis de perles, entrevu par une haute et étroite fenêtre de mosaique verte.

Longtemps elle restait en rèvant sur la terrasse. Elle voulait percer avec son regard la brume, qui maintenant voilait la mer.

Mais elle ne voyait rien, car la nuit comme un rideau bleu tombait sur la terre endormie. De ses yeux mystérieux tombaient deux grosses larmes.

Alors lentement, lentement, elle retournait au palais, qui étincelait sous la lune, plus blanc que la neige des montagnes de son pays.

Derrière elle, ses esclaves chantaient doucement, doucement, les rossignols dans les arbres se taisaient pour écouter.

Elle entendait au loin la plainte de la mer, aussi le vent qui parlait mystérieusement aux fleurs. . . .

Et à travers les palmiers elle voyait les étoiles, . . .

Traduit de l'anglais par l'auteur

The Princess of the Sunflowers

Song to be recited to Music

Listen, Great Lords and Beauteous Ladies, listen to the doleful story of the Princess of the Sunflowers.

The Emperor of Persia had surrendered his daughter, the Princess of the Sunflowers, as hostage to the King of the Golden Isles; thus ended their long-drawn-out wars.

But the Princess did not love the King of the Golden Isles; she loved a young Prince, her countryman.

A young man as pallid as the new moon, who wore a breastplate of ruddy bronze, strewn with white pearls. . . .

Each evening, as the mauve shadows of the great cypresses spread across the rose-marble terrace, the slender captive Princess, escorted by her Negro slaves, came out to watch the sun setting over the sea.

She wore a gown merging the colours of all the flowers, sewn with white pearls which made a tiny delicious sound as she walked, like faraway music. . . .

Amidst her tresses darker than night, two great lilies shone, like glowworms; and from her head hung a sea-coloured scarf, floating behind her like a blue cloud in the evening breeze.

In one small white hand she carried a fan of black feathers; and in the other an immense sunflower with which from time to time she brushed away a red butterfly or bird with golden wings.

The slaves followed her, singing softly. Each of them carried an ivory lyre encrusted with emeralds and pearls; their black hands seemed like shadows on the silver strings.

With their great melancholy eyes they gazed sadly at the sun setting over the sea. They were sick for their homeland.

Their feet were fastened with chains of silver.

Nightingales sang divinely among the trees; and under the tall cypresses red roses seemed asleep.

The air was heavy with the scent of orange blossom, and at the garden's end, in a grove of pomegranates, the rills of a Moorish fountain murmured gaily.

Followed by her Nubian women, the little Princess walked slowly along the terrace; the shadows stretched behind them like sombre ghosts.

Along each side of the terrace the immense, motionless sunflowers stood like soldiers on guard.

On the horizon a pink and mauve sail might have been a strayed butterfly.

The young Princess gazed sadly at the sun as it disappeared beneath the sea—she too was heart-sick for her country.

She longed for her country, for Persia and its burning nights, where she would swoon in the purple-seeming air heavy with the scent of roses, for the soft cooing of the doves in the orange trees; for its blue peacocks, strutting among the myrtles on white and pink silk carpets.

And sometimes, sometimes, the Prince her betrothed would appear to her, his crimson armour, pearl-strewn, rustling, glimpsed through a high, narrow embrasure of green mosaic.

For a long time she remained, daydreaming, on the terrace. She wished that her gaze might pierce the mist which was now veiling the sea.

But she could see nothing, for night like a blue curtain had come down on the sleeping earth. Out of her mysterious eyes two great tears fell. . . .

Then slowly, slowly she returned to the palace, which sparkled under the moon, whiter than the snow on the mountains of her country.

Behind her, her slaves were singing softly, softly; the nightingales in the trees stayed silent to listen.

She heard in the distance the plaint of the sea, and the wind speaking mysteriously to the flowers.

And through the branches of the palm trees she saw the stars.

English version by Edgell Rickword

Far Away

Against a great bronze screen a woman leaned; dressed in a robe of cloth of gold, over which a veil of sea-green gauze embroidered in moon and stars, and strange animals, glittered in the red light of the setting sun — Around the hem of her robe shone large blue stones—stones found at night in the green waters of the Nile—stones found at sunrise in the grey mountains—stones found at noon on the seashore — Around her arms tremble uncut diamonds, and the weight of jewels around her throat makes her breathing a series of sighs — Her fingers seem tired with the heaviness of her rings; from her ears fall two great sapphires — In her pale hand she holds a fan of black & white pearls, and in her dull red hair a great silver bird with outstretched wings — Through the lattice window of the apartment, all the air is blue, tall palm trees throw their violet shadows on the white walls of the palace, and from time to time an orange-coloured bird flies slowly toward the sea — Far out at sea a yellow sail — And on the seashore the slaves sleep or pray to a falling star — Soon, the moon like a great flower appears in the blue night, the palm trees look black and eerie, and the tall cypress trees seem to whisper of Death—

35

Sometimes a white pigeon coos, or the calm night is disturbed by the cry of a peacock, or again, by the long wail of a sleeping slave—

In the room where the woman stands it is now almost dark — Except for a red lamp that burns before a painted idol, there is no light at all—

Against a great bronze screen a woman leaned—

Odette d'Antrevernes
A Fairy Tale for Weary People

I

In the long summer evenings, when the shadows crept slowly over the lawn, and the distant towers of the cathedral turned purple in the setting sun, little Odette d'Antrevernes would steal out from the old grey chateau to listen to the birds murmuring "good night" to one another amongst the trees.

Far away, at the end of the long avenue of fragrant limes, wound the Loire, all amongst the flowery meadows and emerald vineyards, like a wonderful looking-glass reflecting all the sky; and across the river, like an ogre's castle in a fairy tale, frowned the chateau of Luynes, with its round grey turrets and its long, thin windows, so narrow, that scarcely could a princess in distress put forth her little white hand to wave to the true knight that should rescue her from her terrible fate.

Just until the sun disappeared behind the trees, veiled in a crimson cloud, little Odette would remain in the shadowy garden, then quickly and mysteriously she would slip back into the old grey chateau; where, in the long, dim drawing room, before two wax candles, she would find her Aunt Valérie d'Antrevernes embroidering an altar cloth for the little white village church, that one could see across the rose garden from the castle windows.

"Where have you been, my child?" her aunt would ask her, glancing up from the lace altar cloth, that fell around her in a snowy cloud.

And little Odette would reply, in her pretty baby voice: "I have been listening to the birds saying their evening prayers," and then she would sit silently on a faded blue cushion at her aunt's feet, and tell herself fairy stories, until Fortune, her old nurse, should come and carry her off to bed.

Sometimes of an evening the old Curé of Blois-Fleuri would come to visit Madame d'Antrevernes, and little Odette would watch them as they talked, wondering all the while if Monsieur le Curé had really seen God. She had never dared ask.

Her aunt always sat in an immense armchair of faded blue tapestry, embroidered in gold, with the family arms on a background of fleur-de-lys, and her pale, beautiful face, as it bent over the lace altar cloth, made little Odette think of angels and Holy Saints.

Odette had always seen her aunt thus, bending over an altar cloth for God, so whenever she thought of Madame d'Antrevernes it was with a deep reverence that almost approached to awe.

One evening, when little Odette lay awake in her great four-posted bed, watching the firelight dance upon the strange tapestry figures that covered the walls, she heard Fortune, her old nurse, talking to one of the servants. She caught her aunt's name, then her own, and without realising that she was doing wrong, she listened to what Fortune said.

She did not really understand what she heard, for she was

watching the firelight as it shone upon a tall, faded-looking
lady in blue, who was regarding, with outstretched arms,
the sky, which was full of angels. All about the lady, in a field
of red and white flowers, lay sleeping sheep. Her aunt had
once told her that the faded-looking blue lady, whom
Odette had imagined to be the Lady Virgin herself, was Joan
of Arc receiving the message from heaven to deliver France.

So as Odette watched the firelight dancing upon the
faded tapestry, she listened, without knowing that she was
listening to the voice of Fortune, who, in the next room sat
gossiping with another servant.

"She never seems able to forget him," she heard Fortune
say. "Ever since the day that Monsieur le Marquis killed
Monsieur d'Antrevernes in a duel, Madame has never
recovered.

"She had only been married a month, sweet soul, when
her husband was brought home to her dead . . . and so beautiful he looked as he lay in the great hall, his eyes wide open
and smiling, just as if he were still alive. . . . Madame la
Comtesse was in the rose garden at the time with Monsieur
le Curé, no one knew where she was, and when she suddenly
entered the hall, her hands all full of summer roses, and saw
her husband lying dead before her, she gave a terrible cry
and fainted straight away. . . . For days after she hung between
life and death, and then, when she at last got well again, she
always seemed to be thinking of him, always seemed to be
living in the past. Sometimes she would sit for hours in the
garden staring in front of her, and smiling and talking to
herself so that I used to feel afraid. Then a few years later,
when the father and mother of the little Odette were
drowned on their way back from India, Madame seemed to
wake up from her long dream, as it were, and went to Paris
to fetch Mademoiselle Odette from the convent of the Holy
Dove."

Little Odette had fallen asleep berced by the lullaby of the old servant's voice, and when next morning the great yellow sun shone in a shower of gold through the diamond-paned windows of her room, and all the birds in the garden below were rejoicing amidst the trees, little Odette had forgotten the conversation that she had overheard the previous night as she lay awake watching the firelight dancing upon the faded blue gown of the Maid of France.

II

Sometimes of an afternoon Monsieur le Curé de Bois-Fleuri would call at the chateau and ask Blaise, the old butler, whether Mademoiselle Odette d'Antrevernes was at home; and Blaise would smile at Monsieur le Curé and ask him to be seated whilst he went to see.

Then slowly, slowly, Blaise would traverse the great hall, pass under the torn and faded flags that drooped sadly like dead things from the dim oak rafters, and shaking his silver head, and murmuring to himself, he would disappear on the great staircase lined with armour.

And the old Curé would sit musing on the past, his eyes fixed on the torn flags that had once been borne in proud splendour at Pavie and Moncontour.

Then the little Odette in her long lavender-coloured robe would trip like a fairy down the great oak staircase, and making a little curtsey to the Curé, she would take his hand, and together they would walk out into the rose garden that faced the south side of the chateau.

There, by a broken statue, on a low marble seat, they would sit, surrounded by crimson roses, and the Curé, with his soft, low voice, would tell little Odette beautiful stories about the Saints and the Virgin Mary.

But the story that Odette found the most wonderful of all, was the account of the little Bernadette seeing the Holy Virgin in the mountains. This for her was the most beautiful story in the world, and with her quick child's imagination she would picture the little peasant girl Bernadette returning to her parents' humble cottage, when suddenly in a ray of glorious light, the Holy Mary herself appeared on the lonely mountain path, like a beautiful dream.

Oh! how Odette wished that she had been little Bernadette! And she often tried to imagine what the little peasant girl looked like, whether her hair was brown or whether it was gold—and Odette was terribly disappointed when asking the Curé this question, that he only shook his head and said he did not know.

So the days slipped by quietly as on silver wings. Madame d'Antrevernes always in her great blue chair, her altar cloth between her hands, and little Odette on a faded cushion dreaming at her feet.

Then one beautiful evening in August, as little Odette watched the two twin towers of the distant Cathedral flush purple in the setting sun, and the great round dome of St. Martin's church loom like a ripe apricot against the sky, a wonderful idea came to her. She too would seek the Holy Virgin. She too, like little Bernadette, would speak with the Holy Mary, the Mother of the Lord Seigneur Christ.

III

It was the evening of the eventful night.

For one whole week Odette had prayed steadfastly, and now this evening she was going to speak to the Holy Mary in the rose garden, when Aunt Valérie and Fortune, Blaise, and Monsieur le Curé were all fast asleep.

She felt terribly excited as she kissed her aunt good night, and trembling with a beautiful holy fear, she allowed Fortune to undress her and put her to bed.

Then for two long hours she watched the moonlight fall upon the dim blue figure of Joan of Arc, for the little summer fire that Fortune lit of an evening in the great bedroom, had long ago burnt itself out, and now the room was filled with mysterious shadows and strange creakings of furniture, so that it was all Odette could do not to be afraid. At last she heard the gentle rustle of her aunt's gown as she passed her door, and Odette could see the yellow light from Madame d'Antrevernes' candle shine like a little star through the keyhole. Soon afterwards, she heard the slow steps of Blaise crossing the Picture Gallery, and then a sudden silence fell upon the chateau, only broken by the murmuring of the nightingales in the garden.

Odette sat up in her great white bed listening, she felt her heart beating against her nightgown as if it were trying to escape.

Then silently she slipped from her bed, crossed to the window, and looked out.

Perhaps the Virgin was already waiting for her in the garden?

But she saw no one.

Far away she could see a few lights shining like fallen stars in the town of Tours, and through the trees upon the lawn she saw the Loire glittering like an angel's robe beneath the moon.

"How wicked expecting to see the Holy Virgin waiting for me," thought Odette, "it is I that must wait for Her." And fastening a little silver cross about her neck, she noiselessly opened the bedroom door, and found herself standing alone upon the great dark staircase.

To get to the garden it was necessary to cross the Picture

Gallery; for the Picture Gallery was at the top of the great staircase.

Odette trembled as she passed down the long shadowy Gallery where the portraits of her ancestors peered like ghosts from the panelled walls, but she was comforted by the thought that Gabrielle was at the other end.

It was the picture of Gabrielle d'Antrevernes, one of the beauties of the court of Louis XIV, that Odette loved most. And she never tired of looking at the long pale face, the sea-blue eyes, and the dull gold hair capped with pearls, of her beautiful ancestress.

Odette adored the tired languid-looking hands, full of deep red roses, that lay like two dead doves upon the silver brocaded gown, and she would weave beautiful tales about Gabrielle, sitting on her favourite blue cushion, peering up at the portrait, her great eyes lost in thought.

But this evening she did not linger long as her custom was, but with a friendly smile to the beloved Gabrielle she passed by, her little bare feet all a-pit-a-pat, a-pit-a-pat, on the parquet floor.

Then she went down the broad staircase between the pale armour, beneath the faded flags, and so to the glass door that led to the garden.

The door was locked, and oh! the dreadful creak it gave as Odette turned the key! and three little frightened mice rushed helter-skelter tumbling about on the slippery floor.

Odette turned the handle with infinite precaution, and suddenly she found herself alone after midnight in the garden.

Her heart beat so that she thought she was going to die. But oh! how beautiful the garden looked beneath the moon! The roses seemed to look more mysterious by moonlight, their perfume seemed more pure. Odette bent down and kissed a great crimson rose, all sparkling with silver dew, and then quickly she picked a great bouquet of flowers to offer to the Virgin. Some of the flowers were sleeping as she picked them, and Odette thought, with a little thrill of delight, at their joy on awakening and finding themselves on the Holy Mother's breast.

Then, her arms full of flowers, Odette went and knelt down by the low marble seat, where so often Monsieur le Curé had spoken to her of the Saint Mary and of Jesus, her Son. And there, with her eyes fixed upon the stars, she waited . . .

In the trees a nightingale sang so beautifully, that Odette felt the tears come into her eyes, and then far away another bird sang back . . . and then both together, in an ecstasy, mixed their voices in one, and the garden seemed to Odette as if it were paradise.

Suddenly a low moan, like the sound of a breaking heart, made Odette start to her feet.

Could it be that the Holy Mother was in pain? She looked about her.

Yes, there it was again . . . a long, low cry . . . it came from the other side of the wall, it came from the road.

Odette hastily collected the flowers in her hands, and ran swiftly down the avenue of lime trees, her golden hair floating behind her in a little cloud as she ran.

Then once upon the white road, she looked about her expectantly, but there was no one to be seen. The river ran the other side of the road like a silver chain, and far away in the town of Tours a few lights burnt like candles in the dark. She stood still, listening intently; yes, there again, quite, quite close, was the long, sad cry.

Odette ran forward to the river bank from where the sound seemed to come, and there, her face buried in her hands—a woman lay.

"Oh! Oh!" cried the little Odette, the tears rolling down

her cheeks, "the Holy Mother is in pain," and stooping down, she timidly kissed the sobbing woman at her feet.

Then as the woman uncovered her face with her hands, Odette sprang back with a little scream of terror. There, on the grass, amongst the pale white daisies, lay a woman with painted cheeks and flaming hair, a terrible expression was in her eyes.

"Who are you? What do you want?" she asked Odette brutally; and Odette, afraid and trembling, began to sob, hiding her face in her hands so as not to see the dreadful eyes of the woman at her feet.

She felt the woman staring at her, though she did not dare look, then suddenly she heard a laugh, a laugh that froze her blood.

"Why, you have no shoes or stockings," said the woman, in a frenzy of mad laughter. "What are you doing here in your nightgown on the highroads? You've begun early, my dear!" And she rocked herself to and fro, laughing, laughing, laughing, and then suddenly her laughter turned to tears. All her poor thin body shook with terrible sobs; it seemed as if her very heart was breaking.

Odette uncovered her eyes and looked at this sad wreck of a human soul, and an immense unaccountable pity seized her, for suddenly she bent down and kissed the woman on her painted lips.

The woman's sobs grew quieter, as she felt Odette's pure cool mouth upon her burning face. "Who are you?" the woman kept asking her, "Who are you?"

And Odette in her baby voice whispered back, "I have been sent by the Holy Virgin to make you well."

Presently the woman calmed herself, and sat staring at the shining river, as though she had quite forgotten that Odette was beside her.

"Tell me what is the matter," Odette said at length, "and

I will try and help you."

The woman looked at her kindly: "How should you understand what is the matter?" she said, "you, who have always lived with good people, far away from the temptations of the world, what have you to do with the likes of us?"

"I do not understand," said Odette, looking at the woman with great questioning eyes.

"And may you never understand, little one," said the woman, kissing her. "When I was a little girl I heard once some preaching folk talk of God and the Angels. You must be one of them, I think?"

"Oh! no, Oh! no," said Odette, "I am not an angel, but I have been sent by the Holy Mother to save you here tonight."

The woman looked at her curiously. "You only just came in time," she said, and again her eyes strayed towards the river.

"Let me give you this silver cross," said Odette, changing it from her own neck to the woman's. "Keep it always, for it is holy, and is a sign that Jesus came into the world to die for us."

The woman took the cross into her hands, and seemed to weigh it. "Is it really silver?" she asked.

Odette smiled at her, not understanding, "Yes, and is it not beautiful, it was given to me by my mother before she went away to India, I do not remember her giving it me, for I was then only a very little girl, but Aunt Valérie has often told me that when mamma hung it around my neck, she cried, and kissed me, and told me to love the Holy Virgin, for that faith, and love, were the only things that were beautiful in life."

The woman looked at her sadly. "I will keep it in memory of you, little one," she said, "it may bring me luck," and she got up as if to go.

"Will you promise never to do things that the Holy Mary

would not approve of?" asked Odette, taking the woman's hand, and gazing earnestly into her eyes.

"I will try, little one," the woman said, and she bent and kissed Odette passionately; the warm tears falling from her eyes upon Odette's upturned face.

Far away in the East, the day began to dawn, a flush of yellow-like ripe fruit spread slowly across the sky; the birds in the trees called drowsily to one another, and the white daisies by the river side opened their yellow eyes and curtsied to the rising sun.

The woman and Odette stood side by side watching the birth of a new day, then, as a clock struck away across the meadows from some church tower, the woman shivered, and looked down the long white road that followed the river bank.

"I must go," she said.

Odette looked at her. "Where to?" she asked.

"I don't know," answered the woman. "I am going to try and find work—honest work," and taking Odette in her arms she kissed her again and again. "Good-bye, little one," she said, "and since you pray to the Holy Mother, perhaps sometimes you will pray for me."

And then, with a tired, sad step, the woman walked slowly away down the long white road, her shadow falling behind her as though it were her soul.

"Oh Holy Virgin, Mother of Our Lord Seigneur Christ, I thank Thee for having brought me here this night," prayed the little Odette. "Take into Thy protection, dear Mother, this poor woman who has need of Thee, and bring her safely to Thy beautiful Kingdom in Heaven, for the sake of our Lord Jesus. Amen."

Then little Odette returned thoughtfully to the great grey chateau. And as she passed down the long avenue of fragrant lime trees, a thousand thrushes sang deliriously amidst the branches.

But Odette felt somehow changed since last she passed the castle gates. She felt older. For suddenly she realised that Life was not a dream; she realised for the first time, that Life was cruel, that Life was sad, that beyond the beautiful garden in which she dwelt, many millions of people were struggling to live, and sometimes in the struggle for life one failed—like the poor woman by the river bank.

And Odette turned as she walked, and looked behind her, to where, by the roadside, and dying beneath the golden sun, the red roses that she had gathered for the Holy Mother, shone in the morning light like drops of crimson blood.

Harmonie

C'est un soir d'été: les ombres glissent mystérieusement à travers le jardin comme des esprits.

Un lys blanc projette à ses pieds, sur la terre, une ombre grise. Un oiseau, qui chantait doucement dans un cerisier, fait choir de temps en temps, avec ses ailes, une averse de fleurs blanches. Dans une nappe d'eau plus claire qu'un miroir se reflète une étoile d'argent.

Au bord des eaux ont poussé de grands iris pourpres, plus beaux que des visages humains, et sur l'épais gazon, des fuchsias blancs laissent tomber leurs fleurs comme des larmes. D'une vieille muraille de briques éloignée, une pêche mûre tombe avec son mat sur le sol.

Enveloppée d'une ombre bleue et profonde, une corbeille semble devenir, de moment en moment, plus pâle et plus pâle, jusqu'à ce qu'enfin ses fleurs de rêve closent leurs yeux alourdis de sommeil.

Sous un lilas blanc quelques vers luisants brillent comme des primevères en feu.

Un papillon effrayé se cache dans un lys, loin des yeux d'or étincelants d'une grande phalène brune.

Alors un rossignol, dans les rameaux d'un sycomore jaune, égrène son trille profond comme la voix d'un violon lointain.

49

Bientôt une brise légère fait tressaillir l'éventail vert des feuilles de marronniers et éveille les soleils de leur royal assoupissement.

Et les digitales vermeilles agitent leurs fleurs comme des cloches sur la tour d'une cathédrale, tandis que les oeillets carminés, avec des regards ardents, s'inclinent devant les passiflores qui enveloppent, amoureuses, le marbre d'un cadran solaire.

Les violettes se blottissent sour leurs feuilles en forme du coeur, et soupirent . . . parfumant l'air tout entier.

Puis la lune, comme une grande rose blanche, se lève au-dessus de la cime des cyprès et baigne d'une lumière d'argent le visage souriant d'une statue.

Traduit de l'anglais par l'auteur

————————————

Harmony

A summer night; the shadows glide mysteriously across the garden like wraiths.

A white lily casts on the earth beneath it a grey shadow. A bird sings sweetly in a cherry tree; its wings now and then scattering a shower of white petals. In a pool of water more limpid than a mirror a silver star is reflected.

At the edge of the water great purple irises have grown up, more beautiful than human faces, and on the thick turf white fuschias let fall their blossoms like tears. From an old brick wall in the distance, a ripe peach falls to the ground with a dull thud.

Wrapped in a blue, deep shadow, a flowerbed seems each moment to become more and more indistinct, until at last its dream-flowers close their eyes, overburdened with sleep.

Under a white lilac some glowworms shine like fiery primroses.
A frightened butterfly conceals itself in a lily, far from the glittering
gold eyes of a great brown moth.

Then a nightingale, in the branches of a yellow sycamore, pours
out its rich trills like the voice of a distant violin.

Soon the green fans of the chestnut leaves shiver in a breeze and
awake the sunflowers from their regal slumber.

And the crimson foxgloves shake their blossoms like the bells on a
cathedral tower; whilst the scarlet carnations, with ardent glances,
bow towards the passion-flowers which lovingly embrace the
marble plinth of a sun dial.

The violets shrink beneath their heart-shaped leaves and sigh . . .
perfuming all the air around them.

Then the moon, a great white rose, climbs above the crest of the
cypresses and bathes in silver radiance the smiling features of a
statue.

English version by Edgell Rickword

The Legend of Saint Gabrielle

They were all praying, each nun in her own white cell, when the Mother Superior came to them and said: "Come, the Sister Gabrielle is dying, she wishes to say good-bye to you before she goes."

They rose from their knees and followed her silently down long grey corridors, the Mother Superior leading the way with a lighted taper in her hand.

She was a tall majestic woman, with a pale beautiful face, her calm hazel eyes were full of the mystery of prayer.

As the nuns followed her, each one told her rosary; from their pure chaste lips came the soft sound of words spoken to God.

In the garden below the birds were singing, and as they paused outside the dying Sister's door, they could see through an open window the ripe gold of the evening sky, and could smell the sweet scent of the lime trees upon the lawn.

"Enter," said the Mother in a low voice, and together like a troop of white doves they entered the Sister's cell.

The Sister Gabrielle was just sixteen, very beautiful with a face like an angel in some ancient church fresco, she looked too fragile for the world, it seemed as if she were only born to die. Her hands were clasped piously on a volume of devotion, her thin white fingers appeared luminous against the dark cover of the book.

She smiled sweetly at the Mother Superior, and at the group of nuns that stood before her, all stately in their long white robes.

The Sister Angela on seeing her so pale burst into tears.

At the foot of the bed stood an altar draped in antique lace, upon which was placed a silver cross surrounded with Madonna lilies, beyond the altar through the open window the full moon was rising over a garden wet with dew.

A priest with silver hair knelt before the cross supplicating Christ to receive in Paradise the soul of the dying girl.

The nuns fell on their knees about the bed. With eyes closed, and hands clasped they prayed. . . . .

Gabrielle very still seemed to be already dead. A gentle wind played with a spray of jasmine that clung about the window, and stirred the white lace upon the altar.

Suddenly after a long deep silence, from the garden came a soft sound, as of a silken garment trailed lightly over grass, like sweet music it approached, then paused, beneath the window of the dying girl.

Gabrielle opened her eyes wide, she felt as though the supreme moment had come, she trembled with ecstasy and joy, soon now she would see the Holy Virgin, and she would tell Her with her hand in Hers of the great love she had for God.

Then, as she lay panting for breath, appeared in the open window a woman's face, a face so bright and wonderful that Gabrielle thought that she must be already dead.

A blue veil fell from the stranger's head, and the full moon behind her made an aureole for her hair. She leaned through the window, and stretched her hands across the altar and touched the awestruck girl.

"Gabrielle," she murmured, "Gabrielle," and as with lightning rapidity, sweet childhood's memories of Home and she who had made it home, seemed to fill the soul of the dying girl, and the praying nuns watched her Heaven-born smile as she gazed on the beautiful vision, and as with a depth of filial tenderness she whisperingly ejaculated "Mother! Mother!"

Then the woman put out both her hands, and taking Gabrielle silently in her arms, she lifted her through the window, and disappeared with her amidst the trees of the garden.

ॐ

Under the trees the woman paused. "Gabrielle," she said, "Gabrielle speak to me."

But the child's eyes were closed, and she did not move, only her lips smiled as though she were in some exquisite dream.

The woman bent and kissed her passionately, "Awake, awake," she cried.

A bird above in the trees answered the woman's call with a low trill.

Under her feet the ground was carpeted with flowers, violets were in bloom, and here and there amidst tall ferns white foxgloves cast their weeping bells.

She laid Gabrielle down amidst the flowers and chafed her hands.

"My child, my babe," she sobbed, "open your eyes and speak to me and tell me that you are not dead."

But the girl was silent. Only the bird above answered her back with a song.

About them in the great forest all was still. In the sky above the moon sank lower and lower, appearing and disappearing amidst the branches of the trees.

Then at last towards dawn Gabrielle opened her eyes. She did not speak, but remained looking at her mother with her hand in hers.

From afar the Convent bells were ringing, as if for some great rejoicing. . . . .

The sun was high in the sky when Gabrielle died.

୧

In the Convent a wonderful thing had happened. During the night, whilst they were all praying round her bed, the Holy Virgin had come down and carried the Sister Gabrielle away with Her to Heaven to be the bride of Her Son the Lord Christ.

A great joy filled the hearts of all the nuns at the thought that one of their sisters should be deemed worthy to be the bride of Jesus, and from all the countryside came pilgrims to the Convent, to kiss the shrine of Saint Gabrielle.

୧

Through the great forest a mother wandered, and on her breast as though asleep, lay her daughter who was dead.

She did not hear the music of the Convent bells nor did she heed the stones that cut her feet. Amidst the tall trees, solitary in her grief, she walked alone weeping and uncomforted.

Souvenir d'Automne
A Poem in Prose

The leaves are falling by the side of the wood. Slowly, like a flight of lingering birds, they tremble on the brown damp branches, then fall, whirling through the grey air, to lie motionless upon the hard ground, as though stunned from the distance of their fall.

Surely, at the foot of the trees that they once made green, which now in the misty air rise like skeletons from the sodden earth, the leaves are lying as though in Purgatory, waiting for the wind to scatter them to the North, to the South, to the East, to the West, as ships are scattered on the sea by the storm. Yet, whilst they wait, half dead, half living, all gold and strange, upon the dew-white grass, must they not regret the spring, when all the world shone fair, and glad, and new?

Must they not look up with wondering glances to where, not long ago, they hung upon the warm brown boughs, and shook their green, and whispered to the daffodils and violets that grew beneath their shade?

Alas! where now the daffodil? Where now the violet? Then, in that happy time, they did not think it wonderful to feel the first hot kiss of the morning sun, or receive the cooling silver of the evening moon.

Nor did they realise their happiness on those long still nights, when the whole forest, in its mighty strength of living green, vied in numbers with the countless stars; they in their stately pride, forgot that this still sweet life must have its end.

And oh! in that one long month of June, the longing of each branch, as night drew nigh, to have the nightingale to sing amidst its leaves! Each bough would wait, like molten silver wreathed in shining dew; but so late came she, the wondrous nightingale, that the tired, expectant violets closed their leaves and fell. . . . Yet violets never smell so sweet as when they die.

Then all the night, until glad colours filled the widening East, the trees would weep soft tears of dew. For the nightingale sang of the coming of Death, and of great sorrows that the leaves could not then understand, yet which touched them with a feeling of remote and tender grief, as we ourselves are touched by music, yet scarcely knowing why. But now, as they lay prone and still upon the ground, under a sky whiter than a field of snow, they found the interpretation to the nightingale's song, they understood at last the burden of the bird's soul's cry, of the little bird with the passionate warm voice, that had once sung to them of Death and the passing away of all things, and they wondered as they lay, afraid and cold, waiting to be parted from one another by the rising wind, where the nightingale could be.

The Singing Bird & the Moon

I

Every moment the air grew warmer, the sky brighter, the sea more blue.

Above and below, sky and water melted and disappeared in vapoury mist, and between them the air lay so still, that one might almost hear it throb.

Yet alone, a shadow amidst the drifting light, flew a bird with aching heart and drooping wings.

For two long nights and three long days, had she flown over the silent waves, and now on the third night, she knew that she must fall. With wide and frightened eyes she peered about her; never before had she passed across this sea, nor in all her wanderings had she ever seen such transparent clearness in the waves.

Far below her in the depths, grew tall trees of shimmering pink coral, with brittle branches that rocked to and fro lazily with the movement of the sea, long fishes sped swiftly here and there, appearing and disappearing between the jungles of sea anemones, that clung like gorgeously coloured butterflies to the amber-stained rocks, and now and again, deep down upon the yellow sand, gleamed pearls, and little silvery shells.

It was now growing night, slowly the blue sky changed to purple; the air grew chill, and the bird suddenly felt the cold breath of Death upon her warm tired wings, and closing her aching eyes she flew desperately on.

Soon the Moon rose and made a long golden path across the sea; faster and faster sped the bird, with a new-born hope in her heart; perhaps the Moon would have pity on her and show her the way to land.

But her strength gave at each stroke of her wings, like an exhausted swimmer she battled on, for Life was dear.

The stars came out and grouped themselves around the Moon; like numberless servants they seemed to wait upon her royal behest, and the dying bird with one last spark of hope in her breast sang to the Moon and said:

"Royal Lady, if you grant me Life all my sweetest songs shall be for you. With my very soul will I sing your praise. Of your chaste love for the Sun shall be my song. All day will I tell him of your Love, and at night I will fly to you with the warm kisses he lays upon my wings in the morning, and you shall take them from me and carry them back with you to the sky."

The bird ceased exhausted with her song, slower and slower beat her wings, lower and lower she drew nearer the water.

Below her, the dark waves danced so close that she could feel their spray, strange sounds like whispering swept past her through the night, far down in the moving violet of the ocean, the coral trees sighed and murmured—and the fishes that had been glimmering about like silver torches were now no longer to be seen. . . . . . .

Then of a sudden, the Moon turned to white, and hung trembling like a ball of snow above in the misty air, and from her very heart fell a star, it rushed like a flame through the air, then lay glittering and dazzling, floating like an anemone upon the waves.

The weary bird saw it, and with a last effort reached it, and sank upon it half dead from exhaustion.

Then the star with the sleeping bird drifted slowly over the sea, down the long gold road that the Moon had made for them.

II

Now it happened that towards dawn Queen Caridad, the newly wedded wife of the King, stood at her casement window, and looked out with dull hollow eyes over the sea.

The Queen was suffering from insomnia; for many nights she had never known sleep, and so pale and ill looked she, that the physicians of the Palace said, that if some new drug or spell could not be found the Queen must certainly die.

Now, as she stood at sunrise in the pure morning air, she called her favourite slave to her and said:

"Surely I see a strange ship upon the sea?"

And the slave answered her: "Yes, surely there is a sail." And together they stood at the casement watching curiously.

Then as the strange ship drew near to land the Queen fell upon her knees saying:

"I know that Allah has answered my prayer, and tonight I shall sleep."

About the same time, it befell that the guard in the high minaret upon the sands also saw the ship, and summoned his captain, who in like manner spread the report about the town, so that towards noon many people gathered together upon the shore to await the strange vessel.

And behold! as the vessel drew nigh, the people saw a white bird standing upon a star.

With unfurled wings spread out like sails, the wind was driving the strange ship towards the land, and all that saw, marveled and were afraid.

But the Queen, who stood watching at her casement, said to her slaves:

"Run, fetch me this white bird, put it in a silver cage and return speedily."

And the slaves did her bidding, and returned to her, bearing with them the strange white bird, and many hundreds of people followed in long procession the silver cage through the streets.

The Queen herself in her long gold robes of state, went forth to meet it, and taking the cage in her arms returned with it to the Palace, and placed it in her casement window above the sea.

All day long she sat looking at it, seated on eastern cushions, surrounded by her slaves.

At last, towards night, when the Moon rose, the bird began to sing.

At first so sad was its song that the Queen wept, yet so marvelous was the sweetness of its voice, that the people collected under the Palace windows to listen, and many women knelt, thinking it was some God who sang with such divine sweetness.

And below the Palace windows, under the thick shadows of the palms, the merchants came, all white and hooded on their camels, the young men left the bright Bazaars, and the opium dens, and stood entranced at the strange beauty of the bird's song, and the little children too left their mothers' sides, and danced, slowly swaying to and fro, the dance they performed before the idols in the temples on great Feast days.

And in the room where the bird was imprisoned, knelt the Queen in a long green robe, shaded with silvery poppies.

In her white hands she held the cage with the singing bird
high above her head, supplicating Allah to send her Sleep.

Then as the moonlight crept slowly through the open
casement, and fell in a long white ray upon the cage, the bird
spread its wings as though to fly, opening them wide, and
closing them, letting the warmth of the Sun's hot kiss escape
and evaporate amidst the moonlight, and so infinitely sweet
grew its song that the Queen suddenly swayed, and sank
back amidst her cushions, and fell into a dreamless sleep.

III

A year passed by, and the white bird still lived in captivity,
although no longer she dwelt in the silver cage in the
Queen's chamber.

Now she lived in a marble and crystal shrine in the
Temple gardens, with a deep well of sacred water therein
that Buddha himself had blest, where she might dip and
cool her wings as often as she pleased. Throughout all the
land she was worshiped as an idol, and many came from afar
to do her homage.

Every morning the young men of the City brought her
fresh roses, and in the evening young girls in silver veils
would throw her lilies, and so much gold and priceless
gems were offered her as presents, that underneath the
trees around her shrine the earth was bright with jewels.

And all day long the bird faithful to her promise would
sing to the Sun of the Moon, and when night drew nigh and
the shadows fell, she would tell the Moon of the Sun, and
opening the treasured warmth of the Sun's kisses, that lay
beneath her wings, she would give them to the cold Moon
who took them away with her back to the sky when morning broke. And so many and varied were her songs that all

marveled at her wonderful repertoire, and everyone declared that not such another bird existed in all the world.

Then at last (for all things must have an end), one golden morning passed above her head a troop of her own family, and she realised that they were seeking for her, and the bird called to them with tears in her voice, for she was touched that they should have missed her, and were searching the world to find her. But her voice had grown changed and weakened by so much singing, and they passed her by and never heeded the feeble cry she gave.

And her head drooped and she forgot to open her wings to catch the Sun's kisses.

But as noon drew nigh, she heard the sounds of drums, and much laughter mingled with sounds of weeping and wailing, and presently before her shrine appeared a great multitude of people. The procession was headed by an old priest in a white robe, who read a long decree from a piece of parchment before the door of the shrine, and the bird learnt that she was to die, for the people had proved her to be a false god, for that same morning had passed across the sky many birds like her, with voices sweeter than hers, and the people of the City had decided that death should be her fate, for they were tired and ashamed of worshiping a common thing.

And when the bird heard she was to die, she was glad, for she knew now that her soul would escape the bars of her prison, and that she might fly back to the Moon, with one last kiss, and she answered her death sentence with a song so sweet and wonderful that many were moved to tears.

Then they took her and put her in her silver cage again, and in long procession took her to the seashore, to the very place where she had first come. And the Queen watching at her casement window wept for the little bird that had given her sleep.

So they took the cage and set it upon a heap of sticks, and branches and some of the branches were still in flower. Then with a lighted torch they set fire to the wood above the cage and the fire leapt up and danced in the morning light.

And the little bird opened her wings very wide so as to receive the last hot kiss of the Sun, and when the cruel flames touched her wings, she sang, for it seemed to her as though the Sun was embracing her with greater love than ever he had done before, and she tried to think of the Moon's happiness, and so singing she died.

❧

That night as the Moon stole over the silver sands, she came suddenly upon the empty cage of the little bird, that had so loved her, and finding it empty, she stood still in the sky, thinking that the bird had perhaps flown away and was lost. For many minutes her light remained fixed and still on the empty cage, hoping that perhaps by waiting the bird would return with the help of her light. But soon the dawn approached and she knew she could tarry no longer, so she said to the star that was within her:

"Little star, fly swiftly to the silver cage that is upon the seashore, and to the empty shrine in the Temple gardens and fetch me word of the white bird that is lost."

And the star shot through the sky and wandered through the streets of the sleeping City, and it called softly as it passed each tree, "Singing Bird, singing bird," but there came no reply. Then it entered into the silver cage that stood upon the seashore and when it found the few grey ashes of the beautiful white bird, that had once made sails of its wings as they floated over the sea, the star wept exceedingly, and collecting the ashes in the warmth of her soul flew back with them to the Moon.

And when the Moon saw the ashes of the white bird that had so loved her, she hid herself amongst the clouds and refused to shine.

And she wept many tears, for many days, over the land where her little lover used to dwell and the people of that country were glad, for they said that so much rain would be good for their Harvest, and many said by killing the white singing bird of the Temple gardens, the anger of the Gods had been appeased.

Her Dearest Friend

A frail-looking woman in white slowly followed the butler up the twelve steps that led to the drawing room. She trailed with a little frou-frou, over the moss green carpet, and with her lorgnette, stared at a large bronze Venus, that stood obligingly as a hat-stand halfway up the staircase.

"She looks as if she were walking up a mountain," said old Lady Gouch, who was peeping at her from her boudoir.

Lady Gouch was the deafest person in London—she heard nothing, and knew everything — This particular afternoon, she was kept prisoner in her room, having lost her trumpet at Ascot.

It was her birthday today, and she was expecting a few of her school friends for tea. "I remember George IV," she would often begin a conversation, "Also the opening of the Crystal Palace," she would continue, and she would shake her lace cap trimmed with forget-me-not ribbons regretfully, and with faded eyes dream away into the past.

She was one of the very few truthful left in London, and seemed proud of being born in 1828.

"One, two, three, four, five six, she stops," counted Lady Gouch over her spectacles.

The lady in white had stopped before a mirror to touch

her hat, that looked as if it would blow away if there were any draught.

Someone was playing the piano in the drawing room, and she paused to listen, then climbed another stair.

"Seven!" counted Lady Gouch.

The lady though looked annoyed.

"It's Clara," she said to herself, "Clara and Wagner," and she stopped again to count the faults.

"Clara at her worst," she murmured, then as the butler asked her name — "Lady Clio Say," she said and walked into the drawing room.

ॐ

"Who can she be?" asked old Lady Gouch, laying down her Jane Austen.

ॐ

"Well, Clara!"

"Oh! my dear Lady Clio how sweet of you coming." Clara East was a large healthy-looking girl, with big limpid grey eyes, that reminded Lady Clio of "two puddles," the rest of Clara was simply machinery.

"I came to take you on to Lady Victoria Westminster's," said Lady Clio, with a pretty lisp. "I am going there for tea, she asked me and my husband to feed there tonight, and then go on to hear Calvé in *Salome,* but Jack won't go, he can't bear Victoria, he says she gets on his nerves."

"Lady Victoria is really rather tedious," said Clara, "I met her the other evening for the first time since I've been out; she talked about muslin nightgowns and Dora Leith's garden party, and all the time she was making eyes at the Bishop of London."

"Poor Victoria! but stick your hat on like a dear and I'll wait," and Lady Clio sank on to a Persian ottoman and lit a cigarette.

"But I can't go out today," began Clara, "it's Grand-mamma's at home, and she has lost her trumpet, Mamma left for Harrogate this morning and Papa for Buxton, and I am in charge, so you see I can't move. But you must stay for tea with us," continued Clara, "Grandmamma would so like to meet you."

"Your Grandmother was at my wedding," said Lady Clio, "of course being brought up in the country, I knew no one until I married Jack. Having no money we lived peacefully on potatoes and £500 a year in an old grey castle in the North of Ireland, and then unfortunately I met my husband, and we were married an eternity ago at Westminster Abbey."

"Last year," said Clara sympathetically.

Lady Clio lifted her veil from her face, and looked at her reflection in an old French mirror.

A profusion of dull red hair, under a great black hat, a long pale face lit by mysterious-looking eyes that seemed forever changing, a beautiful mouth made to say soft words, or sing strange music; a face that seemed like some wonderful flower found far away in some lonely country by starlight, transported by the explorer and spoiled by its new sur-roundings.

Lady Clio laughed at her reflection a little bitterly.

"I'm awfully changed," she said, "don't you notice it Clara?"

Clara put her head a little to one side, "Yes, I think there is a difference," she decided.

"What is it?" asked Lady Clio curiously.

Clara hesitated. "I think you look wicked," she said at length, "you dress differently now, and it makes you look . . .

comment dirai-je?"

"Oh! if that's all," laughed Lady Clio . . . . . "I should have felt quite annoyed Clara, if you had told me that I looked good."

"I hear the bell!" said Clara getting up and going over to the window.

"Who are coming?" asked Lady Clio.

"Oh! old Lord and Lady Waterport, they are such fun! also Miss Dryd and her son."

"My *dear!*" remarked Lady Clio.

"He is not *really* her son you know, someone gave him to her when he was small. Grandmamma has also invited a Baptist clergyman, who is so old that I am sure he was the first Baptist that ever was, also a Poet who has devoted all his life to writing, and hunting a publisher."

"After your descriptions, I really haven't the courage to stay," said Lady Clio getting up.

"Oh! my dear, you can't *can't* leave me," screamed Clara dramatically, "it would be too, *too* cruel to leave me," and Clara looked beseechingly at Lady Clio.

"Lord and Lady Waterport," announced the butler.

An old man, dressed like a boy of sixteen, followed by a small little old woman, all paint, powder, and grey, walked slowly into the room.

"My dear Lady Waterport!" said Clara effusively.

"How are you?" said Lady Waterport. She had a deep gruff voice, not at all in keeping with her birdlike appearance.

"Very hot today, very warm today, going to be a storm, I feel it," jerked out Lord Waterport to Lady Clio.

Lady Clio smiled artistically, and Clara got up and rang the bell for tea.

"How's your Grandmother?" asked Lady Waterport.

Clara started electrified by her voice.

"Grandmamma's fairly well, thank you," she said, "she

will be here directly."

At that moment, Lady Gouch was wheeled into the drawing room by her maid. She held a new trumpet in each hand, and on her lap slept a little grey kitten.

"My dearest Martha, many many happy returns," began Lady Waterport seizing the new trumpet.

"Seventy-six today," screamed Lady Gouch.

As she was deprived the pleasure of hearing her own voice she always shouted.

"Grandmamma this is Lady Clio Say," said Clara, "you remember you were at her wedding last Spring."

"Of course, of course," said Lady Gouch, "I remember I wore mauve, and left my parasol in the vestry."

Lady Clio smiled vaguely, she had not been listening, but had been designing herself in imagination a tea gown in grey lace. Something soft and transparent to attract Cecil, something that would cost Jack a lot . . . . . .

But Lady Clio's reflections, and Lady Gouch's reminiscence of the opening of the Crystal Palace, were cut short by the arrival of Miss Dryd.

She was a tall thin person with aggressive-looking teeth, and long arms. The rest of her body was discreetly hidden under a long black cloak.

She reminded Lady Clio of a signpost.

"My affectionate wishes," she called down Lady Gouch's trumpet.

"I am glad to see you Jane," said Lady Gouch a little condescendingly, "but where's your son?"

"He has just been appointed Chaplain to Mr. Meason's balloon; he starts in a day or so for the end of the world," said Miss Dryd proudly.

"How very nice for him," said Clara sympathetically.

"Mr. Meason is one of the very few *really* Christian men I know," said Miss Dryd, "and I am sure," she continued, "that his influence will have a most beneficial result with my son."

"What are they going to do when they get there?" asked Clara vaguely.

"Mr. Meason has been engaged by the *Black and White* to post them photographs regularly every week. Also they will try and do a little missionary work on the way," replied Miss Dryd.

"Mr. Theodore Le Vaine," suddenly announced the butler.

"The great Poet!" Lady Gouch shouted to Lady Clio by way of a whisper.

A thin sallow-looking man in a frock coat, with a face not unlike Don Quixote appeared in the doorway. He walked sedately over to Lady Gouch, and in a melancholy voice wished her many happy returns, in a piece of his own unpublished poetry.

Lady Gouch looked delighted, "Wonderful, wonderful," she said nodding her lace cap several times to show her satisfaction.

Clara began busying herself with the tea things.

"I only drink hot water," said Lady Waterport in her man's voice.

"And I like my tea very very weak—mostly milk—" sighed Miss Dryd.

"All tea for me, dear Miss Clara," explained the Poet, "all tea and four lumps."

"And the kitten's milk!" shouted Lady Gouch.

Lady Clio and Lord Waterport were talking about the dreadful class of people that one met at Nice.

"Every one seems to be a jeweller or a jewess," she said.

"And so few of the Nice people are married," said Miss Dryd in her drawing-room voice.

"When Mr. Meason's balloon comes back, you must send your son as missionary to the principal hotels at Nice, Miss

Dryd," said Lady Waterport.

"We would preach together," Miss Dryd replied bravely.

"I know of such nice lodgings—facing the sea," sighed Lord Waterport.

Lady Waterport annihilated her husband with a glance.

"I thought you were at Broadstairs, my dear!" he said by way of self-defence.

"I am afraid I must be going," said Lady Clio getting up.

"It has been such a pleasure to me, to have at last *really* made your acquaintance dear Lady Gouch," she said buttoning her glove.

"Eh! must you go?" said Lady Gouch.

"I have promised to be at Victoria Westminster's at five; it is now half past— I must fly—"

"Oh! I am so sorry if you have missed your train," said Lady Gouch sympathetically.

Clara giggled. "Dearest Grandmamma you don't understand," she said.

"If people *will* call themselves after stations . . . . !" said Lady Waterport in her gruffest voice.

"Good-bye, good-bye," said Lady Clio vaguely, and with her curiously artificial smile, she walked slowly down the long drawing room.

"I will just see you to your motor," said Clara following her.

As soon as they were on the staircase Clara said: "I haven't told you dear, of course it is still a profound secret, but Cecil has asked me to marry him."

"Ah!" said Lady Clio turning quickly towards Clara. "I am so surprised," she said after a moment's pause, "of course, dear, I congratulate you awfully. Cecil is charming— You know of course that he has promised to come to us for Cowes—that is of course dear if you allow him."

"My *dear* with *you!*" said Clara kissing her.

"Au revoir," called Lady Clio from her motor.

Then as the footman asked her where to — "Home," she said.

She could hardly speak, she would have liked to kill Clara, she contented herself however in tearing her pocket-hand-kerchief to pieces.

"I am the most unhappy woman in this city," she sobbed unconsciously imitating her sister-in-law, who was American.

As soon as she arrived at her house, she at once wrote a telegram to Lady Victoria Westminster.

"Should so much enjoy *Salome* tonight dining with rela-tions will come on about ten. Clio."

"I shall wear my new silver and green, and take no notice of Cecil," she said to herself, "Clara is terribly dowdy and with a little tact . . . ."

❦

"Your new friend," said old Lady Gouch to Clara, as soon as her guests had left, "Your new friend reminds me of a serpent!"

The Wavering Disciple
A Fantasia

I

She looked up from the little white-bound copy of the *Imitation of Christ* she had been reading, and fixed her deep eyes plaintively on an oval-framed landscape by Hobbema.

"How sweet to live in a cell," she murmured, "never to have to think about one's clothes, but to be able to sit all day in one's negligée looking out into some shadowy garden, listening to innocent birds and bees, and when night comes to have lovely visions and perhaps see all the beautiful jewellery there must be in heaven!"

And she looked deprecatingly down at the elaborate gown she was wearing; a dress of some soft transparent stuff —of green—resplendent with sequins and embroidery.

Through the open window the sun was setting over the Park. Under the leafy branches of the trees the carriages passed in long, slow procession.

With a little sigh she closed the volume, and leaned her fair hair back against a pink silk cushion, laboriously worked with olive branches and undecided-looking doves.

74

The influence of the book was still quite new to her, she had only chosen it that morning, and had been drawn towards it by the expensive simplicity of the cover. She had scarcely heard of Thomas à Kempis before, or if she had she did not remember. And the book seemed to soothe a sort of yearning she had felt just lately, which she had put down to the stupidity of the London season.

She was interrupted from her reverie by the butler, who came to tell her not enough flowers had been sent for that evening, and she followed him out on to the landing where men were busy hanging chains of smilax and roses, and banking up with blossoms the broad staircase.

She gave a few orders, changed the position of some orchids, and then returned to her room to rest an hour before dressing.

Stretched full length on a sofa, she glanced over the programme of music she had chosen.

"I am so glad I was firm about *Madame Butterfly,*" she murmured, "and all the music now, I think, will go with my dress."

From the wall, in front of where she lay, a nocturne in gold and violet seemed to send forth a languid atmosphere of moon-kissed water and falling stars. A shadowy bridge spanned the picture, whence rapt figures, swathed in Eastern fashion, gazed down into the deep waters as though they were reading there their fate.

Presently a low knock, and her maid Wise entered.

"Monsieur Carl has just arrived from Paris, your Grace," she said.

"Very well, let him come up now," and all the while the coiffeur was arranging her hair after a drawing she had done in Rome from an Etruscan vase, she sat thoughtfully thinking of a simpler life away from all the people who crowded around her, and who exasperated her so; a life of rigid calm, which would make her appear young again.

Her life had always been too elaborate.

She remembered once at Monaco, in their garden over-hanging the sea, pacing to and fro along the terrace trying to resist a terrible temptation; and, clenching her hands in an agony, she had called upon heaven to help her, and to her looking up in her distress the deep sky had appeared almost entirely hidden by masses of pink roses that climbed above, their thin branches caressingly entwined about one another, their heads drooping heavily, as though weighed down by the joy of living, and it seemed then that she had always peered on life through a trellis-work of roses.

And now in a few days she was going to Aix with her husband, and the same weary life would begin again; and closing her eyes she saw it all, just like last year and the year before; the silly water that did her no good, and the Villa des Fleurs where one gambled side by side with the demi-monde of Paris.

With a tired sigh she leaned forward nearer the mirror, and brushed her lips with carmine, and touched her cheeks with rose, and when at last, her toilette ended, she de-scended the broad staircase to receive her guests, she no longer looked the weary blasé woman of the world, but a supremely beautiful girl curiously coiffured, standing smil-ing from under a canopy of Eastern silk, skilfully arranged to protect her from any too strong light.

II

Some words Lord Eastlake had said to her that night as he bade her good-bye rang in her ears, and quite unconsciously they had set themselves to music in her brain, to the melody of a folk song by Grieg.

"I am going away," he had said, "away to a lonely mountain in Scotland, there to lead the simple life."

The Simple Life! And with a rush all her emotions of the afternoon had suddenly returned to her, and acting on an impulse she had gone to her husband and told him that she would not accompany him to Aix just yet, but was going on a little visit to her mother in the country.

And the Duke had seemed glad that she should go.

So half the night she had sat up with *Bradshaw* and *ABC* wondering where she would be happiest, and at last, about three in the morning, she decided that Canterbury would be an ideal place; and although she had never been there, yet in her mind she already saw herself sitting in solitude in some flower-grown garden under the quiet shadow of the Cathedral spire.

Yes! She would live in the utmost simplicity, just a cell all done in grey, with a garden full of pinks and honeysuckle, where she might read Omar and Thomas à Kempis, and Jean Jacques Rousseau, and reflective people like that, who would soothe her and take her out of herself. And, oh! Think of the delight it would be to give up enameling her face, and leave her poor complexion to Nature! And how nice to feel no vermilion on one's lips, and to be able to brush one's hair in the hot morning sun in the garden amongst the birds.

And so her thoughts ran on, until at last, weary, as the opal dawn crept in through the French windows revealing the gold and violet nocturne, with its mystic figures and bridge of dreams, the Duchess fell asleep. But in the morning a disappointment was in store for her. Wise, her maid, who had actually stayed with her a whole year, firmly refused to lend herself to the escapade.

"Sleep in a cell, your Grace?" she indignantly cried. "Never! None of *my* family has ever been in a prison, and no one shall say it was I that was first to bring disgrace upon

the heads of my innocent brothers and sisters. My aged
mother would never leave Guy's Hospital again. Such a
shock to her dropsy would be more than she could bear!"

And for a long time nothing could move her, and it was
only after much persuasion that she consented to go to
Canterbury, and then on the condition that she might sleep
at the hotel.

The Duchess passed an entrancing week preparing for
her *Vita Nuova,* as she was pleased to call it, and Wise was
kept terribly busy packing tea gowns, parasols, and reli-
gious-looking books.

A biography of Lucrezia Borgia and another of Lord
Randolph Churchill were put in to fill up space, and on
Tuesday night everything seemed quite ready for their early
start the following morning.

They left next morning at daybreak for Canterbury in a
motorcar.

III

"No, mum, I am sorry to say we have no cells on our books
just at present" was the house agent's chilling reply to her
anxious enquiries.

This pale lady, whose face was draped about with a long
emerald-green veil, and who wore an entire owl in her hat,
made him feel uneasy.

She peered at him despairingly through her motor glasses.

"No cell!" she murmured, and turning to Wise, who stood
on the doorstep gazing up respectfully at the Cathedral
towers, "What is to become of us?" she asked.

The young man seemed touched at her disappointment.

"Would a summerhouse do?" he suggested.

"What sort?" asked the Duchess, ignoring Wise, whose

teeth chattered at the idea.

"Well, mum, it belongs to the gardens of the Curfew House, but I don't think it would be let without the rest of the estate."

How perfect! The Curfew House! A garden! A summer-house! The Duchess revived. She would take the whole property, and Wise should sleep on the premises so as to be near her. And next day before ten o'clock the Duchess was out pulling the rusty bell of the Curfew House.

Through the scroll iron gates she could see the old house long and low, with its lattice windows peeping out amidst a labyrinth of tumbling wisteria and jasmine.

She felt almost faint with happiness at the prospect of living here. Perhaps, after all, this was her true vocation, to lead the religious life, and wild thoughts of taking the veil and entering a Convent flashed through her mind.

Would the Duke object? She wondered, and even if he did, no doubt it might somehow be arranged. "He might come and stay with me sometimes from Saturday to Monday," she told herself. "And I am sure he would not care to come oftener, because in a Convent there are so many rules."

And the summerhouse? Words failed.

It was round, carved with smiling Cupids and Satyrs in old moss-covered stone, with a pointed door, and a cupola which made one feel infinitely religious, and outside ran a façade like a Greek temple, of thin fluted columns, through which one beheld the garden all beautiful with flowers.

For the next ten days the Duchess was forced to stay at the hotel, whilst the necessary alterations took place.

She had the open spaces of the summerhouse filled in with glass, and from a slender rod, running round the cupola above, fixed grey silk curtains, that fell in long straight folds to the ground, giving a peaceful and monastic air to the room.

The Duchess was charmed with the effect, and even Wise, who peeped in cautiously, admitted that it looked "very stylish."

"Austere, you mean," the Duchess corrected her.

There was no furniture in the apartment save a feather mattress, and a music stool was the only chair; all the little luxuries that they had fetched with them from town were stored away in the house.

It was a radiantly fine Saturday afternoon when the Duchess moved in.

They walked over from the hotel, followed by a porter wheeling their small luggage on a hand-barrow.

Wise followed reluctantly; she was sorry to go from the hotel, where she had started a little intrigue of her own. Besides, the idea of sleeping alone at night in an old house frightened her. Clad in sombre garments of some thick woollen texture, she followed the Duchess and the hand-barrow, walking very slowly, as though she were preceded by a hearse.

The whole of that first day the Duchess spent immobile in a hammock, with eyes closed, listening rapturously to the bird and insect life around her.

The Cathedral towers were visible over the garden wall, soaring up to heaven, more beautiful than she had imagined even in her wildest dreams, seen through the fragile twisted branches of a magnolia tree in flower.

The garden, too, was full of fruit. Yellow apricots and rose-red peaches crept side by side over trellis-work along the garden walls, and a fig tree, as though outraged in modesty, essayed to stretch its branches, breaking with ripe fruit across a path, to protect from profane eyes a cowering nymph.

It was delicious to repose there languorously, with half-closed eyes, and as evening fell the bells from the Cathedral chimed melodiously, and the sky quite suddenly turned all gold. The flowers closed themselves, and the bees left off their work and circled through the air, humming drowsily, as though discussing the flowers they had visited during the day, and presently the moon rose, and cast aside her veils, silvering the hair of the cowering nymph—a white blot amidst the dusk.

But the Duchess had fallen asleep, and was dreaming restlessly of the last reception she had been to at Marlborough House, when suddenly, in the midst of an imaginary curtsey, she awoke with limbs cold and stiff from so long a siesta. For a moment she remained still wondering where she was.

All round her stretched the dew-drenched grass, with the wind rustling amongst the leaves, and somewhere high above her in a tree (behind which the moon was hiding) a night bird called rapturously for its mate.

She sat up and ran her hands over her hair, setting it straight.

"I must look awful," she said, "and how dreadfully hungry I feel. Oh, dear! How nice a little supper at the Savoy would be, and just to meet a few people one knows! I feel quite afraid out here all by myself; everything looks so weird." And shivering with cold she got up and went into the cell.

For a long time she could find no matches, and when at last she managed to light a lamp, a quantity of moths flew in and swarmed around her. The Duchess, almost in tears, was forced to put out the light and, seating herself on the feather mattress, opened as best she might a tin of foie gras, which she devoured hungrily.

"How very wrong of Wise leaving me like this," she said, as soon as she had finished. "I must go and see what has become of her," and crossing the garden, she made towards the house, darkly hidden amongst the trees.

The sunflowers as she passed them looked fast asleep, and the sprightly columbines, all black and white, seemed to be holding converse with the stars.

The front door of the Curfew House was locked, so was the back, and all the windows were securely fastened with shutters.

"O, what shall I do?" moaned the Duchess. "Must I spend the whole night here in the garden? Whatever shall I look like in the morning?" And sitting down on the doorstep she began to cry.

A window cautiously opened, and a gleam of firelight flickering on the ceiling above made the Duchess look up.

There in her nightgown, her hair delicately twisted in curl papers, stood Wise, looking fearfully out into the night.

"Advance if you dare," she said in a voice weak with fear. "There are men and dogs in the house; come a step nearer and I fire!"

"Oh, Wise! Wise!" sobbed the Duchess.

"Is that you, your Grace? May the Holy Saints be praised! I thought it was burglars." And leaning her head against the shutters, Wise burst into nervous hysterics.

"Oh, God knows all I have suffered this night, your Grace," she wailed, "the house is haunted and full of strange tapping noises, just as though someone kept advancing to kill me with a stick." And unable to proceed further, she stood in the window wringing her hands.

"Be quiet, Wise," said the Duchess sharply. "Control yourself and let me in. I am dying with cold; make haste, come down and unbolt the door."

And when at last the Duchess found herself comfortably seated in an opera cloak before the fire, with a cup of strong beef tea, she began to consider the position.

Clearly they could not stay another night in the place, she would go mad if she did. It was dreadfully unfortunate having the house for three months, but that could not be helped. The best thing she could do now was to join the Duke at Aix.

"A wife's duty is with her husband," she told herself, "and it was very wrong of me leaving George to face alone all the temptations there are bound to be where he is" (forgetting that only yesterday she had been making plans to leave him altogether and enter a Convent).

And presently when she felt a little calmer she sat down and wrote to her husband:—

My dear George,—I am leaving today for Aix after a charming visit to mamma. She regretted so much your not being with us.

I will keep all my news until I arrive. As you will see by the post-mark, I am staying at Canterbury with my old governess—Miss Cowper.

Good-bye, dear; I hope you have not been gambling very much.

Your affectionate wife.

P.S.—I am returning to London from here to get more clothes.

"I wouldn't for the world he should know the truth," she said, "or he would certainly be cynical at my expense, and I suppose I must arrange a little falsehood for mamma. It would be dreadful if people heard about it, or if it got into the papers. I shall give Wise a new dress to keep her quiet."

But some ominous words of Wise's troubled her, and she remained pondering them some time before she fell asleep.

"I must tell my sister about this night's adventure," Wise had said; "she is an actress, and plays gloomy parts on tour."

And when at length the Duchess fell asleep, she dreamt she saw a girl sitting at a spinning-wheel, clad in a faded rose-coloured robe, and the girl's eyes were full of tears as though some great misfortune were upon her, and when the Duchess awoke the room smelt sweet with lavender, and the spinning-wheel of her dreams stood with empty shuttle, just as she had seen it in her sleep.

"I wonder if that was really a ghost," she murmured. "What a pretty frock the girl was wearing, I must try to remember it, and have one made like it," and crossing to the spinning-wheel she examined it closely. The name "Mélisande" was engraved upon it, almost obliterated with time. "Mélisande, I wonder who you were, and who lived here," she mused. "But I must think about breakfast now," she added, looking at her watch.

Outside the sun had already risen, the garden was sparkling with fresh dew, the flowers were unfolding, the bees were busy, the birds were awake.

Between the Maréchal Niel roses the cell appeared grey and stately—a fairy temple in the early morning light.

"It looks just like a Watteau," said the Duchess.

A Study in Opal

She glanced stealthily at the sleeping Bishop, and opened
her dressing case noiselessly, her hands fluttered undecid-
edly between her powder-puff and a mysterious-looking
china box. Would she have time for both?

A subtle scent of hyacinth, mingled with some other
perfume indefinable, wafted from the scarlet leather
fittings.

A *Bradshaw*, a *Life of Mary Magdalen*, vellum bound,
some French novels, and an ostrich feather fan, disclosed
themselves for one hurried instant to the admiring sun-
beams.

The train was slowing down; it was foolish of her to have
left her complexion to the last moment. Powder alone must
suffice.

"I look anyhow," she murmured, closing her dressing
case with a snap.

She was wearing white, with an opal and diamond crucifix
at her breast, her black straw hat weighed down on one side
by a cluster of deep pink roses.

A toilette, a little elaborate perhaps for a Bishop's bride.

"Wake up, Bob!" she said, addressing her husband. "We
are just there, and oh!" she murmured, pressing nervously a

bouquet of lily of the valley to her heart, "they have gone and put up bunting."

The Bishop let down the window, and leaned out.

"This is the first time they have done such a thing," he began, but stopped, fearing to hurt his wife's sensitiveness.

"You mean poor Ethel?" she enquired, her voice discreetly soft.

"Yes, dear. We remained at home for the honeymoon. It was spring time, I remember. She preferred the garden, she said."

"So this has been your first real honeymoon?" Lady Henrietta Worthing asked.

"And I hope it will not be my last," replied the Bishop unconsciously.

She hummed a few bars of Brahms to show that she had not noticed, and just then the train stopped.

Nearly the whole of the little old-world town of St. Catherine-in-the-Marsh had turned out to greet them. Lady Henrietta did her best to endure the ordeal stoically. All these good clergymen and their families were, she found, a wee bit tiresome; and when two unattractive-looking babies demanded a kiss, she began almost to repent her marriage; the Bishop had let her in for more than she had bargained for. A child came forward and presented her with a flamboyant bouquet of sweet william and phlox.

Lady Henrietta acknowledged the tribute with a gracious smile. It gave her a pleasant feeling of royalty, but what a pity the child had not brought orchids, and why were phlox and sweet william, when they weren't white, such a wicked shade of pink? She gave the flowers to her maid to hold, and busied herself with her parasol and dressing bag.

There were flags flying all down the High Street, and the Union Jack drooped lazily from the Cathedral tower.

"It was quite unnecessary making any fuss," Lady Henrietta

said, "and why Mrs. Granger hangs an Austrian flag from her drawing-room window to welcome us I am too tired to imagine."

The Palace was some distance from the station, and in sight of Lady Henrietta's former beautiful estate, Forby Park.

For one moment, as she passed her gates, an intense longing seized her to descend from the Bishop's brougham and return home.

"Good-bye," she murmured to her husband, just as she used to do, "and I shall expect you to lunch on Sunday?"

She divined her garden behind the high brick wall, the herbaceous borders brilliant with Indian carnations, and that new climbing tea rose—Madame Sarah Bernhardt—that must surely have reached her boudoir window by now.

There were her dogs, too, and her pigeons; she could hear them cooing in the cedar trees on the lawn.

"Ah!" she never realised when she married the Bishop what it meant to give up Forby.

True, she had always coveted the Palace. To have a Cathedral growing at the foot of one's garden was an immense attraction.

She could run in and out of it all day now, and perhaps she might be allowed to fit herself up a little boudoir above the organ loft.

Delicious to sit there amidst the stone saints and feel oneself a sinner, whilst the sunlight streaming through the rose window dyed one's face to an unearthly green. Surely in such an atmosphere the soul must expand, become transfigured. And what is more becoming than to wear one's soul in one's eyes, on one's lips? And there existed a dressmaker in Paris, rue St. Honoré, to her knowledge, who made the most ethereal hats. Hats! Halos rather.

She sighed at her thoughts.

"Are you tired dear?" the Bishop asked her. "I am afraid

we looked at too many pictures. I myself do not feel quite
the usual good health I am wont to enjoy; my mind is too full
of frescoes. I must get Dr. Brice to give me a sound tonic,
and will renounce the pleasure of taking early celebration
just yet. The dear Canon shall officiate for me just a little
longer." And he settled himself comfortably in the corner of
the carriage, with a gentle purr, his hands folded together,
stiffly pious, in the manner of the shrine erected to his pre-
decessor, the lamented Bishop Greening, in the Cathedral
nave.

The sun had set when they reached the Palace.

The Cathedral rose in strong delicate outline, black
against a luminous green sky.

Pigeons brooded softly from their homes amidst the gar-
goyles. A patch of ruddy light lingered an instant in a niche
where once a saint had stood.

Lady Henrietta descended, and paused a moment, lost in
contemplation of her new abode.

The house dated from the fourteenth century; a thing of
joy with its steep tiled roof and mullioned windows. Flagstone pavements circled around it, moss-grown, and worn
with the passage of many feet.

Paths bordered by yew and box led away on all sides into
blue twilight, and at even intervals aged dragons stared
fixedly before them, their thin stone limbs chained fast by
trails of pale convolvulus and velvet-leaved clematis.

The sound of bolts being drawn back in the heavily spiked
door, and Clinton, the butler, and Mrs. Forrest, the housekeeper, loomed in the hall welcoming them in.

Like some dim interior by Van Dyck perhaps, but not
what she was accustomed to. Lady Henrietta chafed. Why
were there no lights? Why was not tea waiting?

She went up the shadowy staircase to the drawing room
resolute to change everything. If only she could get some of

the Forby servants back. Carter! What a treasure he had been to her! And then there was Sampson, too; an admirable woman. The seven years she had been housemaid at Forby she had let fall but one Dresden harlequin, a record to be proud of. And it was a pleasure to see the way she had cried over it. If it had been her own child she could not have displayed greater emotion.

Lady Henrietta arranged herself luxuriously on a sofa in the big bay window. How deliciously near the Cathedral seemed to her across the garden. She could almost hear the bells breathe! Surely mediaeval witchcraft had wrought those winged demons, and the cool hands of Saints fashioned the hooded forms that seemed to soar. And how sweet the garden was in the twilight. The Bishop had always loved old-fashioned flowers, and the air was full of the scent of them. Hollyhocks! They reminded her of the picture books she used to look at when she was a child. And columbines too! fantastic things! And those dusky fires under the ilex trees, what were they? She opened the casement wider and leaned out. Marigolds! And just beyond these were roses fading paler from moment to moment, as the night closed over them.

She turned as her husband entered. He came up softly and stood beside her.

"Henrietta," he said tenderly, "does it make you happy to be here?"

"Of course, Bob," she answered. Then after a short silence, during which the first star appeared in the deepening sky.

"But you mustn't forget your promise dear, before we married, to give me the key of the Cathedral. I shall so love running in and out at odd hours. I will go there often, after sunset, when it is all still and shadowy, and perhaps one enchanted evening the stones will tell me their secrets."

The Bishop looked bewildered. "How curious you are, Henrietta. I don't think I always understand you?"

"Give me the key now," she pleaded. "I should like to go and say one little prayer before I dress for dinner."

The Bishop stooped down to kiss her, but she had not removed her hat.

"You know I like you better without that great hat," he complained, as he handed her the key.

"I mean to wear a Mantilla in future," she told him. "Madame de Verneuil, the Belgian Minister's wife, says the sun stains one's hair gold if one sits in it long enough."

A faint sound behind them, like a ghost coughing, made the Bishop turn.

Framed in the open doorway the wrinkled face of Mrs. Forrest, the housekeeper, showed fantastically in the expiring light. Her black dress was one with the shadows, she seemed to have no body, her features alone were visible as though floating in space.

"Might I speak to your Lordship," she enquired, "I am sorry to disturb," she added, "but it is a matter of importance."

Her pale countenance swam from side to side like some curious fish risen from the violet depths of the sea.

"What a creepy expression," Lady Henrietta remarked, "go, dear, and see what she wants."

The Bishop followed the housekeeper into the library, lit at one end by a heavily shaded lamp.

"Well, Mrs. Forrest," he asked, peering kindly at her through his pince-nez, "nothing wrong, I hope."

She came towards him, her aged hands clasped crosswise upon her breast.

"Your Lordship," she began, her voice quavering with emotion, "your late wife—Miss Ethel—whom I nursed from the day she came into this world, walks."

"Walks!" echoed the Bishop.

"Her spirit. Last evening as I was taking down the linen from the cupboard in Queen Mary's Chamber, I heard just behind me a sigh, so sad, so sorrowful it was, that I *knew* it was from some other world.... 'She has come back,' I said to myself. 'The Queen has returned.' And I looked round slowly, my arms extended just as they were. There, standing behind me, almost as if woven into the tapestry on the wall, stood a lady. Her outstretched hands shone from within, so that I could count each blue vein. Her face at first sight was misty, covered with some fine veil as it might be, and she stood there palpitating, as though caught in the meshes of the tapestry, like a soft white bird. 'It is Queen Mary,' I said, signing the air, and falling upon my knees, and when I looked again the veil had lifted from the lady's face, and I knew that it was Miss Ethel that had come back."

Mrs. Forrest, overcome, sank down on the broad window seat, her trembling hands resting on her knees, her head bowed forward. The night wind blowing from the garden stirred the ribbons in her cap.

The Bishop, much moved, paced thoughtfully to and fro.

"Bob! Bob!" called Lady Henrietta from the darkness of the garden, "what are you doing indoors? Come out and admire the stars!"

"Henrietta," the Bishop said, going out to her, "I want you to do something for me. Don't question me, dear, I will tell you everything tomorrow, only tonight I want you to sleep at Forby."

"Sleep at Forby!" Lady Henrietta, who had been placing a trail of Virginia creeper into the jaws of the aged dragon, turned to her husband in astonishment.

"Bob!" she said dramatically, "don't tell me there is something wrong with the drains!"

"Ask me nothing tonight, dear," the Bishop said, taking her hand. "I will go now and order the brougham for you.

You will, of course, take your maid, and the groom can sleep at Forby if you wish and fetch you back again early in the morning."

"But there will be no linen aired," she objected. "The house is shut up; I should feel very nervous sleeping there without the usual servants."

The Cathedral clock struck ten as she spoke.

"It's monstrous, Bob," she said, smiling mysteriously, "to drive your wife out of doors at such an hour! However, dear, as there's going to be a lovely moon, I don't very much mind, I shall spend the night in the garden listening to the owls."

He left her standing under the black yew trees, her thin jewelled hand resting on the lean ribs of the starved dragon.

"What can be wrong," she wondered, "but I must go and get out of this frock if I am to spend a night in the garden."

She found her maid packing a bag for her with ill-disguised annoyance.

"You needn't wear such a persecuted expression, Jason," Lady Henrietta remarked. "I shall not need a night-dress. Get me out my blue linen gown, with the Greek-key border, and give me my opal necklace. I am going to spend the night in the garden at Forby."

With an expression of horror, Jason did as she was bid. She would give notice in the morning, she decided, if anything further were required of her.

Although Lady Henrietta was going to pass the night alone in a deserted garden she could not resist the temptation of illuminating delicately her cheeks with rose, and spraying her breast with Syringa and Frangipanni.

This done, she descended in stateliness to the hall, drawing on as she came a pair of long tan gauntlets, fringed round the edges with purple silk.

The Bishop stood waiting for her at the foot of the stairs.

"Good night, dear love," he said, kissing her, "trust me

till next we meet!"

As the carriage rolled away through the Palace gates Lady Henrietta felicitated herself on possessing neither a jealous nor a curious temperament.

"Few women," she reflected, "would do as much as this without pestering their husbands with a thousand questions."

Arrived at Forby, she alighted at the little green door in the west wall that led to the gardens.

"Go on to the house, Jason," she commanded her maid, "and do your best to be comfortable. Try and bring me some tea at six o'clock tomorrow morning, and be careful the dogs don't snap at you in the dark."

There was a blue dreaminess in the garden that reminded her of Corot. She wandered on down the chestnut avenue, stopping now and then to admire the distant hills, that glimmered like fairyland across the Park.

If Pan—most fascinating of gods—would only reveal himself to her suddenly from amidst the heavy drooping foliage, with clash of cymbals and barbaric dance!

She wondered vaguely what she would say to him, supposing he should come. "I would show him my garden," she decided, "and get him to inscribe his name in my autograph book, and, in return, perhaps I might give him that photograph of myself as a Bacchante in my tulle ball gown, with vine leaves in my hair."

She stood a moment breathless, watching the summer wind sway the tall cuckoo flowers from side to side.

How peaceful it was! And she was a Bishop's wife! All her life now would pass by quietly as on silver wings. That distant Cathedral tower, that seemed to link earth with heaven, was practically hers! When she died she would have a beautiful window placed there in her memory. Ah! If Burne-Jones had been still alive she would have entrusted it to him; for the moment she could not recollect anyone first-rate who painted on glass. She would have to enquire. "And I should naturally like to see the window," she murmured. "It might be executed in my lifetime, and Bob will see that it is properly placed when I am gone."

She paused in her walk before a herbaceous border. "Those Réjane tea-roses require manure," she remarked, sighing pensively as she gazed up at the stars.

"If I had realised I was spending a night *à la belle étoile,* I would have removed my corsets," she reflected.

In the distance the Cathedral bells chimed the hour.

Opening an ivory fan painted by Conder, she held it slant-wise across the night. It pleased her to watch whole planets gleam between the fragile sticks. A flash of summer lightning sped across the sky. Far off the sound of dogs complaining to the moon broke the stillness.

She seated herself on a garden chair and considered the distant glimpse of the house through the trees.

What was she to do with Forby? Clearly it was a white elephant now that she was married. Yet she could not bear to part with it, and the idea of turning it into a Cottage Hospital, as the Bishop suggested, made her shudder. There would be operations perhaps going on in her drawing room, a room she had so identified with herself (a theatre she believed they called it), and in her morning room, where she had passed so many happy hours, poor frightened children, huddled together, would wait their turn, just as she had seen people at the seaside sitting uncomfortably on the steps of bathing machines expectant for the door to open.

"Swe-e-e-et," twittered a bird in its sleep above her head.

"Angel-thing," Lady Henrietta exclaimed. "Pet!" and for a moment she regretted that she had no children of her own, "though motherhood is often unbecoming," she consoled herself with the thought. Poor Mary Hungerford for instance! Five babies had spoiled her coral cheeks and dulled her Venetian hair.

She looked down at her own willowy figure closely swathed in blue, and caressed with her pointed fingers the cold opals at her throat.

How green they flashed!

She looked up at the sky. It was already morning.

"I shall be glad of some tea after my vigil," she murmured, straightening adroitly her hair.

Away in the country a cock crew. A soft flush of light spread calmly from the East, sending back mysteriously the colour of the earth.

The trees cast aside the violet shawls they had wrapped about themselves during the night, and stood in the clear morning shivering, the pale green of their leaves against the bluey-whiteness of the dawn. And out of the dark shadows crept crimson, and saffron, purple, and gold, and fainter colours, indefinable yet soft notes of white, and grey, and lilac, bathed with pearly beads of dew.

Lady Henrietta uttered a little cry of delight. "Nectarines!" she flew towards the wall. "Strawberries," she crushed them beneath her slippers!

A brown owl brushed past her, blinking at the warm light, but Lady Henrietta heeded him not. She stooped down to the rich perfumed earth, intent as any bird of the air on finding her morning food.

How delicious the strawberries tasted.

"If I had only known how near to me they were," she thought, "I might have enjoyed my night so much more!"

At that moment Jason appeared, looking far from amiable, meandering through the flowery grass, a tea tray extended before her.

She wore a distinguished-looking toque with an osprey,

and a stylish black dress, which her late mistress, the
Duchess of Cirencester, had given her when she gave up
mourning for the Duke, and married Mr. Baillie, of Cambus
O'May.

Advancing cautiously towards Lady Henrietta, she stood
for a moment criticising what she considered the unlady-
like position of kneeling in a strawberry bed.

"Can she be saying her prayers?" Jason enquired of herself,
"or is she after the strawberries?" She stood still watching.
As a servant she never neglected an opportunity of studying
her employers. Her thin shadow stretched to where her
mistress knelt; the waving osprey plumes on her head
struck her as coquettish mirrored on the ground.

Lady Henrietta turned guiltily. What could be more innocent than to eat strawberries, and yet somehow she felt as
though she had been spied upon.

"Good morning, Jason," she said, with a faint smile, "I
hope you slept comfortably."

Jason placed the tray on the path, annihilating as she did
so inestimable quantities of insects.

"I have not closed my eyes, your Ladyship," she said, in
her most uncomplaining voice. "I passed the night, my head
propped against an empty birdcage, reading an old number
of *Who's Who* I found in the servants' hall. Your Ladyship has
not slept either, I see," she remarked severely, "this morning
your Ladyship is as pale as an albatross!"

"Don't Jason, you make me tremble," Lady Henrietta
explained. "Do you think I am going to have an illness?" she
enquired anxiously.

Jason struck an attitude, like a figure on an Egyptian vase.
"I am no prophetess, your Ladyship," she humbly informed
her, "but if I was in your health I would take two glasses of
port wine and go to bed."

Lady Henrietta drank her tea.

"Order the carriage to come round as soon as possible," she commanded, "I will return to the Palace."

Jason was an alarmist, and half an hour later, as Lady Henrietta sped through the misty lanes, in the comfort of her smart new brougham, she began to feel reassured about herself and wondered vaguely what curious news the Bishop could have for her. "Capricious dear!" she summed the Bishop up.

At the Cathedral door she dismissed the carriage, and entered a moment to say her morning prayer.

How hard the cushions were in the Palace pew! It was difficult to keep one's thoughts fixed when one's hassock was stamping Genoese velvet on one's knees!

The organist was practising something for Sunday. Lady Henrietta, from where she knelt, could see his head appearing above the loft.

"He is fair," she murmured, "and looks quite a boy. I wonder whether he is blind? It is so much more touching when they are!"

Her large eyes became sorrowful at the thought. The azure light from the rose window flooded her slim figure, turning the blue linen of her gown to a deeper shade. She slipped off her gloves, and spread her hands out into the cool colour. It reminded her of the Grotto at Capri.

Nine silvery notes from the Cathedral tower told her of breakfast.

Her emotions delicately vibrating, Lady Henrietta crossed in stately leisure the flagstone path that led to the Palace.

She pictured as she went the different fashioned shoes that must have passed over these very stones since the days of Richard Cœur de Lion, and glanced down at her own fragile feet, cased in varnished slippers, sparkling modishly with steel rosettes.

Here and there she paused to pluck some dewy rose, or

spray of pastoral eglantine.

A few loose flowers, sweetly scented beside her on the snowy breakfast cloth (amidst green Chelsea cups and saucers and old Jacobean silver), made the early morning easier to bear.

But could anything have happened at the Palace in her absence?

Every blind drawn down; the house seemed asleep.

Was it fancy? But Lady Henrietta thought she detected an expression of mockery creep through the veiled windows, as though some horrid monster watched her approach through half-closed lids. The blue tiled roof cast sombre shadows across her path, making furrows that appeared to frown. The pigeons, sunning themselves on the gables and in the eaves, brooded over some long story she could not understand.

She examined her watch. Surely she was not deceived in the hour? No! It was after nine.

Hurrying forward she entered the house through the library window. Where were the servants? Why were the blinds still down? It was like entering a pyramid of the dead. She crossed to the windows and shook back the curtains. That was better! The sunlight streamed in dazzling the venerable eyes of some Bishop long since dead, whose portrait hung on the wall opposite.

Where was her husband, though?

She seated herself at the piano and commenced to play.

The Bishop's room was just above; he would hear her and come down.

She sang the serenade from *La Tosca*, "To the Dawn," but the thought of breakfast, and re-arranging the drawing room, deprived the words of any meaning.

She broke off in the midst.

Mrs. Forrest was standing before her on the threshold,

a withered hand held up warningly.

"Hush! your Ladyship," she said, coming towards her. "Something terrible has happened."

Lady Henrietta rose to her feet with a little cry.

"Speak!" Her hand pressed her heart. Marguerite Gautier had stood thus when her lover left her.

"His Lordship has gone to join Miss Ethel in glory," the old woman solemnly pronounced.

"You cannot mean he is dead?" Lady Henrietta gasped. Her fingers wound about her jewelled crucifix. Surely a stone was missing? She bent her eyes to see.

"Yes, your Ladyship, his soul flew away from him in the night as he slept. They say," she added dreamily, "that it takes a soul twenty-four hours to arrive in Purgatory. He must be halfway there now," she murmured, looking at her watch.

"Take me to him," Lady Henrietta said, shaking Mrs. Forrest by the arm, for the old woman stared before her as though she beheld visions.

"He is in Queen Mary's chamber," the housekeeper said, leading the way, and together they went to where the Bishop was.

Lady Henrietta paused, amazed, upon the threshold.

The Bishop was seated in a high armchair of Spanish leather, grimly carved, robed in the full vestments of the Church.

Through the drawn tapestry curtains the sunlight streamed softly, making the jewels in his mitre glow with subdued fire. His hands, clasped upon his breast, enfolded a silver cross.

"Like a tired king in a Maeterlinck play." Lady Henrietta felt shocked at herself for the thought.

"But why," she asked in a church whisper, "did he put on this Popish attire?"

Her interest seemed greater than her grief.

"If it please your Ladyship," Mrs. Forrest answered, "he came to lay a ghost."

"A ghost!" Lady Henrietta was incredulous.

"Miss Ethel, his first wife, came to take him away from your Ladyship. Hers was always a jealous nature. Even as a child she would never allow anyone to tamper with her property."

"Tamper with her property?" Lady Henrietta looked at the Bishop.

"What you tell me is quite absurd," she said at length, "and if the occasion were not so sad, I should be amused. His Lordship, now I think of it, complained several times of not feeling himself. His mind was full of frescoes, he said, and I heard him express a wish just after we had déjeuner at Ventimiglia Railway Station that he had not touched the rainbow-coloured entrée. I did my best to dissuade him from it at the time, but he would not listen to me, and I daresay it was that that killed him."

She seated herself uncomfortably on the edge of a chair, and burst into a torrent of nervous weeping.

It did seem hard to be left so rapidly, and only a few hours ago she had quite made up her mind that she should die first.

It was upsetting, too, to think that if she wanted it she would have to erect her own window in the Cathedral, in memory of herself.

"Lucky I ordered a black velvet dinner gown," she sobbed, "and may a widow wear pearls?"

"I suppose I shall return to Forby," she thought presently, when she had become calmer and more accustomed to her loss. "There is nothing," she philosophically mused, "like possessing a thing to find out its true worth, and now, the first sharp spasm over, I almost believe I prefer returning to my own charming house to residing here. I esteemed the dear Bishop, rather than loved him; I may confess it now in the privacy of my heart! And I shall consider the happiest days of my life were those Sundays he lunched with me at Forby."

With a gentle frou-frou of skirts, Lady Henrietta rose from her chair and crossed to the window, where a full-blown rose cast arabesques across the blind. Breaking it off, she returned to her husband's side and placed it upon his lips.

"There," she murmured, "there!" in the voice she sometimes used when arranging a troublesome lock of hair. Kneeling down an instant, she cast her eyes in supplication to heaven, demanding Poppies, Forgetfulness. But how could she pray satisfactorily with a distracting eight-legged thing on a beam above likely to fall on her at any moment?

"I must fortify myself with sleep," she told herself, rising from her knees. "I shall require all my strength to help me through these next few days. They are likely to be very trying."

Then with cautious delicate tread she tiptoed from the room, holding her skirts closely about her.

At the door she turned and looked back.

She would not enter again . . . and sighing twice painfully she passed out.

❦

(*Letter from the Lady Henrietta Worthing to the Marchioness of Hungerford.*)

Telegrams: Ripley.
Station: St. Catherine-in-the-Marsh.

Forby Park,
Dorsetshire,
Friday, September 19th.

MY DEAR FRIEND,

Your sweet letter of condolence so long unanswered has been weighing on my mind.

Prostration at my irreparable loss must be my sole excuse. Your beautiful words of comfort, and the little volume of French Maxims, have sustained me during these days of most trying sorrow.

Thanks, kind dear, for the invitation to your house at Cowes. I know well how you would look after me, and spoil me, but I feel no wish for the present to leave the seclusion of my beloved Forby. Besides, Cowes is hardly the place for a grief like mine. I should meet too many people I know.

I have been meditating lately a plan to perpetuate my husband's memory. You, dear, a great patroness of arts, the Isabella d'Este of our day, could perhaps assist me in finding what I seek. It is my desire to place a window in the Cathedral in his honour, a *double* one, so that when I die my name may be also coupled by posterity with his imperishable one.

Could you, dear Mary, help me to select an artist worthy of so lofty an undertaking?

Do you remember the *Samuel* window Mrs. Goring erected at York to her husband's memory? It was imposing. The delicious pink of the angels' wings deepening towards the ends, and the radiant purple of little Samuel's girdle, and all the rest a symphony of ravishing flesh tints and Seraphims I have not yet forgotten.

I have in mind a *Jacob's Ladder* for poor Bob. My *own* window I want decorated with a St. Francis. What a charming person St. Francis was; devoted to gardens and birds and the Simple Life that has always held so great an attraction for me. I do not wonder that God sent him Stigmas. If any saint deserved them it was he.

Forby is lovely with the autumn tints; I have seldom seen the Park look statelier than just now. The chestnut avenue is turning from orange to Venetian red, and the garden is a wilderness of beauty.

My poor soul aches sometimes very bitterly, and when the last swallow is on the wing I shall take myself to Biarritz, where the Empress has sweetly asked me to pass a month alone with her in the healing balm of her garden. Her gentle presence would soothe the throbbing of the sorest wound.

Good-bye dear, do not forget to make enquiries about a really reliable artist. I shall not rest until the windows are accomplished. Your ever affectionate friend,

HENRIETTA WORTHING.

P.S.—I am taking a little house in London after Christmas. My love to your babies.

A Tragedy in Green

TO
THE INSPIRER OF THE TRAGEDY,
SIR COLERIDGE KENNARD

Pierrot: Pierrette, you are looking so serious today, I am going to invent you a story; a perfectly heartless story.

Pierrette (her hands clasped): Oh! Dearest Pierrot, I love stories, especially the kind that make one cry! I enjoy to cry, besides I have the sweetest pocket-handkerchiefs—real Venetian Point . . .

Pierrot: My incomprehensible Pierrette, there will be no need for that; it's a Funny Story.

Pierrette (bursting into tears): A Funny Story! How vulgar!

Pierrot (kissing her): Rose of my life! you already weep?

In her bedroom at Seven Stones Castle, Lady Georgia Blueharnis awaited the dinner gong. She had arrived only that evening, leaving her husband unavoidably detained at the Foreign Office; and this was the second halting place on her Autumn round of visits.

"My dress is far too beautiful to be down first," she murmured to herself, "and it was foolish of me to have dressed so soon."

She was wearing a gown in three shades of green, with

profusions of falling crystals, her dull red hair shrouded in a silver net. As she moved, a diamond crucifix swung lightly from an almost imperceptible chain.

"I am a work of art," she sighed, "and this evening I feel nearly as wicked as Herodias."

It was one of Lady Georgia's habits to find equivalents for all her worser feelings in the Bible.

Smiling with the candour of a Mona Liza she looked about her. In the penumbra from the mullioned windows the tapestried walls looked dim and aërie. Here, and there, a unicorn fed unconcernedly in a flowery field, or sometimes a virgin passed, with neck bowed, absorbed in the perusal of an austere Missal, her threadbare feet very pale on the ice-blue grass. On a bracket, above the bed, stood a little box-wood image of a saint, with a very long neck, holding a sheaf of lilies, and behind the dressing table, white as an altar, steps rose to a platform in the bay window, where a luxurious sofa, piled with many cushions, stood solitary, offering rest and a view of the stars.

Lady Georgia sighed again. "If only," she said, addressing herself to the nearest, and most sympathetic unicorn, "if only something would happen! Why did I marry a man who is forever busy compiling his *Memoirs,* or doing nothing at the Foreign Office all day, ah! why? To live solely for dress, or for what people so curiously misname 'pleasure,' to be spoken of invariably as 'the aesthetic Lady Georgia,' even when one is only wearing a muslin blouse, and a bunch of primroses, is surely not to exhaust all the possible emotions of life?" and piqued by the unicorn's unintelligent silence, she added sadly: "Silly beast, graze on!"

Far away, over the gardens, from the village of Seven Stones the church clock struck eight. Eight silver notes like the petals falling from a rose. On the terrace below she could see the upturned face of a statue smiling at her through the dusk. Above, the sky was thick with stars, little fragments of the moon, blown away by the wind; and through the open windows came a scent of flowers—a subtle mingling of wallflower and stock—wafted in upon the night air in overpowering persistence.

Lady Georgia's irritation against life increased.

The scent of certain flowers often made her unhappy, and an alliance of stock and wallflowers was more than she could bear.

"Why is that horrid Mrs. Gaveston staying here?" she complained, "the sort of woman who will play Debussy before lunch when every village child knows that he should be only listened to by electric light, and why did Genevieve pack my Vauvenargues—the only man that has ever really understood me—in my riding skirt at the bottom of my box? Still perhaps a little poetry will compose me almost as well, something about daffodils, I think, and tired, tired shepherds, asleep under great big trees, with a glimpse of Mount Etna through the branches."

And she crossed over to the bookcase, moving slowly, her hands clasped above her head, carefully, to avoid crushing her Greek coiffure.

There were a great many books, and the choice was embarrassing.

Lady Georgia read the titles over, murmuring them to herself: *Fabulous Histories of Maids of Honour, The Home Life of Lucrezia Borgia, Mrs. Turrit's Adventures in the Harz Mountains, The Cult of Osiris, Prayers for Pierrot,* and then suddenly her eyes fell on a curious-looking book, bound in ivory-coloured parchment.

At the sight of the book—she could scarcely explain it— her heart stood still. Trembling, she stretched out a hand towards it, setting as she did so, a-shiver, like breaking icicles, the crystals on her gown. Something warned her not to touch it, she felt the book would wield a fatal influence over her life, over the lives perhaps of others . . .

For a moment her hands fluttered like two lost doves towards the motherly linen back of *Mrs. Turrit;* she would find safety there. But no! the very shape of the little parchment-bound volume fascinated her, and realising the futility of resistance, with trembling fingers she untied the strings.

The book seemed of great age, it felt damp to the touch, and as Lady Georgia opened the cover she expectantly shuddered.

At first, one might have supposed it to be an unused diary, it seemed to contain only a number of blank pages, stained at the edges to the faint gold of autumn leaves, but in the centre, a small red blot, dusky, and not unlike a drop of blood, made Lady Georgia scream beneath her breath. Above the blot, in a sinister and quivering hand, was written in Gothic characters: *Spells and Incantations.*

Starting exquisitely, Lady Georgia glanced fearfully over her shoulder.

In the long mirror behind her, she could see her willowy form, misty as a painting by Carrière, and even at such a moment, she could not help admiring the sheen of her dressing-gold gown as it caught the light or the ravishing angle of her arm. "It's no use . . ."

In the dim flare of candles, the tapestried walls lurked with shadows. Here, and there, the white form of a unicorn feeding unconcernedly in a flowery field, made startling the summer twilight, and walking demurely through the tall grasses strange virgins passed in never ceasing chain, with necks bowed, absorbed in the perusal of austere Missals, their threadbare feet very pale on the ice-blue grass. While, through the open windows, over the still branches of the trees, the full moon rose languidly, like a heavy flower, tired with the little moon, still unborn, she carried with her.

Her nerves, delicately vibrating, with a fear of the Unknown, withal pleasurable, Lady Georgia sank down amidst the piled-up cushions, determined to read every-thing, missing not even the preface should there so happen to be one. Her attention was arrested from the very first. With breathless interest she read the opening chapter, written in the same wizardlike hand, and entitled: "On the Invocation of Devils."

Enthralled, she passed on to the second which dealt minutely with "The Conjuring up of Spooks and of Divers Furious Beasts," but it was the third chapter with the simple heading: "On the Overthrowing and Upsetting of Public Buildings, and the Houses of Private Individuals," which made her pause and look up. After a brief interval in which it would be difficult to follow her dazzling train of thought Lady Georgia continued to read: "It is better," began the chapter, "and in order to ensure complete success, that the building selected be situated within a short distance of lake, river, or sea." Here followed an amiable dissertation on XV century architecture, in which the author spoke in glowing terms of Cathedrals, Mosques, and Venetian palaces, men-tioning casually, that he himself had, after an unsettled boyhood, lived for many years in Paris, in the belfry of the Church of Saint Julian des Pauvres. The chapter, after pleas-ant gossip, went on to say that: "A firm faith in, and a proper conviction of the uselessness, architecturally or otherwise, of the said building, was essential in bringing about its irrevocable doom."

Then followed a number of mystic words, and the direc-tions for the casting of the spell. The book came impressively to an abrupt end with the words, "Amen Selah!"

The sound of the dinner gong at that moment brought Lady Georgia to reality.

Radiant with happy purpose, she rose from her depth of

cushions, shaking out, as she did so, her green skirts as might a bird its wings. Her plans were made . . . she had only to write them down in her engagement book. Proceeding mechanically to the dressing table, with the aid of Poudre Rachel, and spirits of roses, she obliterated with expert fingers all traces of her recent emotion.

"I want to be beautiful tonight" she murmured "and just a trifle abandoned-looking for I think I caught sight of Captain Dimsdale in the hall, as I came upstairs. I do hope so, superb pet!" An entrancing vision stretched before her. At last her prayer was granted, she was to be a *force* in the world. Emperors should quail before her. With the edge of her handkerchief she waved aside the last trace of powder from her nose. But before turning her attention to various little places abroad—Mrs. Gaveston's villa at Cannes for instance —she decided there was work for her to do nearer home. A few of her friends' town houses must be seen to first, and hurriedly, she made the following little list on the fly leaf of a *Life of St. Rose de Lima.*

> Madame Lemoine
> The Dowager Lady Hoop
> Jane Seafairer
> Lady Lydia Lamp
> Mr. Pecklesnaff
> Miss Venetia Yorking
> Princess Doria Grimaldi
> Rachel and Emily Blueharnis.

"Nobody could possibly know what the list means," she said to herself as she went downstairs, "anybody would think it a dinner list, if (which is not very probable) they had the curiosity to peep into St. Rose's *Life;* although poor little Mr. Pecklesnaff amongst eight women . . . !" and she laughed.

But her initial experiment? Who could for a moment doubt it? She would overturn the Foreign Office into the lake in St. James's Park, and at the same time debarrass herself of her husband.

II

It was a Tuesday afternoon, a Tuesday more drowsy than any Tuesday he could remember, in all his long reign at the Foreign Office, and Lord Blueharnis nodded in his efforts to keep awake. He was writing to his old friend General Love-lock to thank him for a rare cactus that had arrived that morning from the East. "The flower is most exceptional," he wrote, "It is a most exceptional flower."

Decidedly there was something peculiar in the atmosphere that day, the air was so still, it seemed bewitched.

In St. James's Park, the swans brooded motionless under the shadow of the trees, and a woman, hidden behind a green parasol, had sat by the water's edge since early morning, as though too indolent to walk away.

There was something sinister Lord Blueharnis thought in that motionless green parasol; the very shape of it troubled him. From the adjoining room the faint sound of "presses" opening and shutting broke the drowsy stillness. For twenty years he had been familiar with the sound, and just now it soothed him.

"It is a most exceptional flower," and again his eyes strayed towards the park.

"Monstrous," he thought, "to be detained in London at this time of year; there was Georgia gadding about in Scot-land and enjoying herself . . . but was she in Scotland? She had not written for over a week; it was most extraordinary."

A young man entered the room with a sheaf of papers.

"Any news?" asked Lord Blueharnis.

"They have caught King Bomba at last," murmured the young man vaguely, "but excuse me, Sir, have you noticed the colour of the sky?"

"Is it not the colour of the seventh veil of that remarkable Greek dancer, whom I once had the pleasure of seeing perform at 'Tea' in your mother's drawing room? To be more precise, is the sky not blue?"

It was one of Lord Blueharnis's idiosyncrasies to address those younger than himself in the tones of a duke in a Jacobean melodrama.

"The sky is *not* blue," answered the young man in a strange voice, "it is vert de paon," and with that he withdrew as quietly as he came. The sky had in truth undergone a sudden metamorphosis.

A gold and peacock-green cloud, like an Eastern prayer carpet, was advancing leisurely towards St. James's Park; it seemed for a moment as though it would shatter itself against the tower of Westminster Cathedral, but swooping cautiously aside avoided the contact. Following at a short distance behind, two small clouds in close conspiracy threaded their way; and these two small clouds were the most beautiful Lord Blueharnis had ever seen. They were of all the colours of an Indian twilight, fringed at the edges with a deep rim of silver fire.

"If a painter were to paint such a sky," reflected Lord Blueharnis, "everybody would say it was quite incredible."

A golden gloom sweeping up from the direction of the Embankment added to the strange feeling of unreality, but what astonished Lord Blueharnis most, was the extraordinary steely glint on the lake in St. James's Park. He noticed also that the green parasol was no longer there. The wind, suddenly rising, began to sway the yielding trees in a riotous valse, and bore off triumphantly the last loose petals of the summer roses, scattering them like a handful of gems through the park. An ilex tree, unassailable, one would have supposed, by the virtue of size, and age, became infected by the mad music of the storm, and lifting up a ponderous branch, proceeded to perform a pas de seul; her myriad leaves, fluttering about her in the wind, like the ribbons on a monster crinoline, oblivious both of her dignity as the oldest tree in the park, and of the little white hands of the Queen who had planted her there, two hundred years ago.

"Can it be a portent of war?" asked Lord Blueharnis anxiously. "It would be too tiresome if it were, for I have not had a change since Easter."

It was now no longer possible to see and turning on the electric light, his Lordship sat down to complete his letter. Outside, the wind and lightning were terrific, and a gentle swaying of the floor gave him the impression of being in a train de luxe; and this reminded him of a curious incident that had once befallen him in a train de luxe, between Seville and Madrid, and with a sigh he took down a sumptuous folio, in which for some time, he had been writing his reminiscences.

Whenever Lord Blueharnis took down his reminiscences he sighed, for what were reminiscences but a vain crying after a youth that had slipped beyond recall?

After a few moments he began to write.

"It was a gorgeous evening, I remember," he began, "I was second attaché in Madrid in those days, and . . . it was a corridor train. Sh! but I anticipate. I had noticed on the platform at Seville, a lady—deeply veiled. Distinguished? She was the most distinguished creature I had ever seen; even under her heavy veil and long dust-cloak. I think she first attracted my attention as she stooped to buy some violets, and wild cyclamen, from a little barefooted child. There was something regal about her as she stooped, and irresistibly she suggested to me Alcestis. But her nationality was what puzzled me, and hoping to gain a clue I followed her to the bookstall. Evidently, she, on her side, had been studying me through her veil, and not impossibly suspecting my motive, made her choice of papers expressly for my benefit; for it was decidedly complex.

"*Gil Blas, The Morning Post, Der Vaterland, Osservatore Romano, Los Madrileños,* a Russian novel by Maxim Gorki, and a Turkish periodical, with a gorgeous supplement of a massacre, printed in two colours—red and blue. As she turned away from the bookstall laden, I saw the gleam of her eyes beneath her veil, and . . . they were the most magnetic eyes; eyes once seen never forgotten. By the time the train arrived—which was quite an hour late—I was enormously intrigued to find out who my Alcestis could be. To my delight she installed herself in the next compartment to mine, and through the thin partition I could hear her directing the porter where to place her luggage in a voice of quite exceptional beauty. It was a gorgeous evening, and after a while, we both watched the sun dip below the mountains from the corridor; when it had quite disappeared, she sighed a long fluttering sigh—and returned to her seat to watch the moon rise from the other side. Alas, the pity of it! the opportunity to ingratiate myself seemed to have forever gone. Soon afterwards, I am ashamed to say I fell asleep. My dreams took me to the Opéra Comique and as I slept I seemed to hear Gluck's music, and the voice of Alcestis chanting at the cavern's mouth, 'Divinité du Styx.' I awoke suddenly; surely there could be no mistaking it . . . the low penetrating voice of a woman, and the soft thrum-thrum of a guitar. *She* was evidently singing. Tiptoe I stole out into the corridor, and as I stood there spellbound, watching her, I think I may have experienced some of the emotion the Magi felt, when they first saw the Madonna's face. Seated in the

full light of the Spanish moon, the intensely white moonlight of Spain, her veil raised, a guitar pressed against her
breast, her eyes drinking in as she sang, the shadowy mountains, the orange-clad hills, sat the Empress of ———."

III

It was Easter. Six months had gone by since the "sad affair of
the Foreign Office"; and in the solitude of a landaulette Lady
Georgia sat turning over the leaves of her husband's newly
published *Memoirs,* the only thing saved out of the débris
with the exception of an agate tie-pin which nobody had yet
claimed. Instinctively she glanced at the last page. "Tiptoe I
stole out into the corridor," she read, "and as I stood there
spellbound, watching her, I think I may have experienced
some of the emotion the Magi felt, when they first saw the
Madonna's face. Seated in the full light of the Spanish moon,
the intensely white moonlight of Spain, her veil raised, a
guitar pressed against her breast, her eyes drinking in as she
sang, the shadowy mountains, the orange-clad hills, sat the
Empress of ———."

"Poor man!" murmured Lady Georgia, "he was evidently
writing when the blow came, but how like him to leave off
where he did!"

She was looking her very best, in an immense mourning
hat, turned up behind, and caught together by a bunch of
black violets almost as large as pansies; a penitent-looking
feather waved about her left ear, whilst an audacious veil,
thickly speckled with velvet, was thrown over all. This veil,
which scarcely suggested widowhood, was the only little
licence she allowed herself; the rest of her gown was of the
strictest rigour; "decorous" her maid had described it as she
put it on.

She closed the book impatiently. "I am miserable, utterly, utterly miserable," she complained. "How Blueharnis has made me suffer . . . how much renounce! Oh! the weariness of a long mourning! but I suppose I should feel thankful that Rachel and Emily went about the same time, it will save beginning all over again. And to think I may not wear green without making everyone look shocked or surprised for at least another six months. Green!" she cried lyrically, "colour—mine! I do not care about you in trees, nor do I like you in vineyards, or meadows, and least of all at sea! But in *rooms,* in *carpets,* in *brocades,* and oh! in *gowns,* you are the only colour that brings to me content. When I remember that green négligé at Clotilde's, the tears start to my eyes. Consider! a négligé is as short-lived as a flower, shorter sometimes, for sleeves will alter in a night! and this particular négligé was so perishable, a puff of air would have destroyed it. The subtlest thing! I see it now . . . neither blue nor green, like the eggshell of a thrush, with frail clusters of Hops, falling from the arms, and the model that wore it—an ugly plain little thing—had silver vine leaves in her hair. Oh! if I have committed any sin (and my conscience does not tell me that I have), I have been cruelly and bitterly punished." She leaned back, tired a little, with the excess of her emotion. After a moment, she picked up one, of two unopened letters that lay beside her. Of one she knew the writing, it was from Captain Dimsdale, the other looked dull and official.

Breaking the seal she read.

Dearest Queen,

Your handwriting is beautiful. It is both mystical, and emotional, but like all really beautiful things, it does not reveal itself at once. I gather you ask me to dine with you tonight at a quarter to eight? Nothing could give me greater pleasure.

Guy Dimsdale

"Enchanting being! how he understands me!" Lady Georgia sighed.

At the second letter she smiled; the exquisitely candid smile of the Gioconda . . . The letter was to ask her whether she would lay the foundation stone of the new Foreign Office.

"I think I must!" she exclaimed, "it will be a delightful situation, and I shall enjoy it immensely. There will be solemn speeches, and I shall be presented with a trowel and a bouquet of flowers. I suppose I must be in half-mourning —violet chiffon, and emeralds, and an elaborate sunshade; it will be the greatest fun!"

At Stanhope Gate, Lady Georgia leaned forward with languid interest. Men were removing the last stones that were left standing of the Princess Doria Grimaldi's house.

"It was the least successful of all my attempts, but certainly it made the most perfect ruin," she mused, "and now I have an uninterrupted view of the Park."

"Where next your ladyship?" asked her chauffeur.

"Back to Clotilde's."

But at the corner of Dover Street she changed her mind.

After all one must pay the price of one's actions—that was life, as a widow "green" would be a scandal, the négligé must be renounced. The punishment seemed out of all proportion to the offence.

"Clotilde's, your ladyship?"

"No, to the Oratory," she called faintly.

Lady Appledore's Mésalliance
An Artificial Pastoral

Although the Venetian blinds were down in the white-paneled room where Wildred sat, it was impossible to shut the sunlight entirely out.

It came in hesitatingly through the thick silk draperies, and, pale as a moonbeam, slid over the Persian carpet, warily like a cat.

He did not notice it for some time, he was too much engrossed in his own sorrow, but presently he felt the sun's warm touch creep through his body, and with a weary sigh he lifted up his head.

"Hullo!" he exclaimed, as he noticed the sun shining upon his hands. "What are you doing here? Didn't they tell you that I was not at home today? What are the use of Venetian blinds, I should like to know?" and going over to the long windows, he pulled the lazily dropping blinds up with a rush.

"After all, what's the use of sitting in the dark?" he murmured.

The brilliant afternoon had brought out streams of carriages, that wound slowly down Piccadilly towards the Park. From behind the hood of each carriage fluttered parasols, like delicate full-blown flowers, and beyond the high green railings, on the opposite side of the way, the trees in St. James's Park had begun to join their shadows in faint patterns upon the grass.

"At this hour tomorrow," thought Wildred, "I shall have started my new life. Oh! what will it feel like, I wonder, watering Orchids, and making wreaths of Stephanotis for Lord Appledore's grave? However, I would sooner do that," he murmured, "than stay in town, and go into some sordid city office, and bear the humiliation of being gradually dropped by my former friends."

He looked round the dainty white and gold room, and there were tears in his eyes.

Life seemed so hard just then!

On a grand piano stood an open piece of music by Debussy, and in long vases, everywhere scattered about the room, breathed drooping pink Tea-roses, amidst profusions of Wisteria.

A large packing case stood in the centre of the room; how unsympathetic, how out of keeping it looked!

"Still I must make a beginning," he told himself, and stooping down he began to fill the box with favourite books and music.

"I don't suppose that there will be a piano there," he said. "How should there be? And I must just take my simplest clothes, these silk pyjamas are far too smart, but then I can't afford to buy woollen ones, so here goes!" and he rolled them up round a family photograph of a lady in Court dress.

"Poor Aunt Cynthia! she is about the only one of them who would sympathize with my experiment, and even she might be a little horrified!" and with a sigh of regret he gently laid a large paper copy of Maeterlinck's *Ariane et Barbe-Bleue* into the ugly wooden case.

When the packing was finished, he dressed himself carefully and went round to Half Moon Street to fetch his cousin, Sir George Liss.

He had already engaged a table for dinner at the Ritz.

"After all why shouldn't I spend my last evening as I like, and as George pays for the Opera box, it would be really mean if I took him to dine with me at Lockhart's, and it's all through him, too, that I got the place."

☙

"I have a letter from Lady Appledore about you," Sir George Liss said to him at dinner.

"She is in terrible trouble about a mauve and black Orchid that she fears is going to die, and her Maréchal Niel Roses, she says, were not nearly so fine last year as the year before."

"Her mauve and black Orchids shall be my special care," murmured Wildred as he sipped his champagne. "I remember seeing her with them once at a Court ball, she had a long chain of them falling from her shoulder in a shower over her train, and her husband was trying to act as a paling, to prevent them from being crushed."

"Yes, do be gentle with the Orchids, and try to make the Roses big again," his cousin begged him; "remember if anything goes wrong, it is I that will be blamed for having recommended you."

They arrived at Covent Garden just as Isolde was swallowing the Love potion, and all through the stormy music that followed, Wildred sat with closed eyes allowing the music to pierce through him.

How frightful his situation really was! Apparently he was practically penniless; until everything was settled, which might take another six months, he had no income at all. To have had everything, to lose everything. . . .

He leaned his long pale face upon his hand.

How beautiful the music was, and this was probably the last time he would ever come here. How hard it was to give up all that made life worth living. . . .

He turned as his cousin touched his arm.

"Look!" Sir George said, "do you see the woman with the aigrette in the box opposite?"

"You mean the woman fanning herself?"

"Yes. That is Lady Appledore."

"How very amusing!" said Wildred, peering at her through his opera glasses.

౯

Nobody else got out at Minster-le-Hope.

It was one of those ideal-looking little villages, that one sometimes passes through in the train, but where one never stops at. The Foxgloves grew right down on to the line, amidst high bracken and ferns, and all around stretched a magnificent oak forest. The name "Minster-le-Hope" was written in dissipated-looking scarlet geraniums, that were doing their best to escape into a bed of violet-coloured Poppies.

With a sense of relief, Wildred got down from the hot third-class carriage.

How exquisite it was to breathe the pure evening air!

The white vapour from the engine rose falteringly into the paling sky; on all sides glimmered the wild Broom, and the Gorse.

"How iniquitous it is!"

There was no conveyance of any kind at the station.

"We have so few visitors at Minster-le-Hope," the station master explained, "and then they only come to visit the church. Oliver Cromwell's mother is buried there, and there's also a niece of a Cabinet Minister, who died only the other day."

"I have not come sight-seeing," Wildred said, "but want to get to Wiston, Lady Appledore's place, which is, I believe, about three miles away."

"Are you the new gardener?" the station master enquired. Wildred stared. "Yes, but how should you know?"

The station master laughed. "All Minster-le-Hope knewed you was coming," he explained.

"Then do tell me where I can get a carriage," asked Wildred.

"A carriage! Young man, there is no such thing, but if she is not using it, you may borrow Mrs. Maley's cart from the Horse & Crown."

"How very tiresome," thought Wildred, and leaving his box at the station, he set out on foot for the village.

It was not very far. He could see the Norman tower of the church through the dark foliage of the trees. A little beyond shone lights from cottage windows.

He had no difficulty in finding the place, and whilst the cart was being got ready, he seated himself on a wooden bench outside the inn, and watched the bats rush past, and the distant hills grow fainter and fainter in the failing light.

The moon had risen when at last they started.

A signpost, looking like a very thin Pierrot, pointed a white arm towards Wiston.

Wildred was too much occupied with his own thoughts to notice the country through which they passed. He recollected a certain evening in Berlin, at a dinner at the English Embassy, he had told a diplomat's wife that should he ever be obliged to earn his living he would become a gardener. And she had laughed, and thought the idea charming. "Delicious," she had said, "to pass one's life arranging nothing more dangerous than flowers! Think of the joy of choosing a colour scheme for an herbaceous border! and the beneficial result of a quiet mind to the complexion, which is so difficult to acquire in Berlin!"

How little he had thought then that one day his idle words would come true! And now that they had, his mind misgave him dreadfully... and besides, he had to admit it, he felt absurdly nervous of meeting Bartholomew, the head gardener. Whatever would he be like? and what should they talk about? "I hope I shan't see very much of him," he murmured, "and I wonder, if he is married, whether I ought to leave cards on his wife?"

The cart jolted through a plantation of young larch trees, that hung their drooping branches so low over the road that their soft green twigs, wet with dew, swept their faces, on, out on to a misty common where a windmill slowly turned, and turned, like a revolving crucifix.

Suddenly they stopped before a long red brick wall.

"Is there anything wrong with the horse?" Wildred enquired.

"The horse is healthy enough!" the driver answered. "These are the gardens."

Wildred sprang down, glad that the drive had come to an end. The driver rang a rusty-looking bell.

Over the garden wall, that seemed very old, Wildred could see the tops of fruit trees, through which the stars were shining. The wall ran along the highroad for nearly a quarter of a mile, and seemed to end in a clock tower, that was probably the stables.

The sound of a key, turning in the little green door in the wall, made him look round.

A pretty, but untidily coiffed girl peeped cautiously out.

"What do you want?" she asked, "if it's father he's on duty and cannot come."

"I'm the new gardener," answered Wildred.

"Oh indeed, then come in."

She opened the door wide, and stood aside to let him pass.

"Carry the box across to the room above the potting-shed," she told the driver, and turning to Wildred: "Come now, and have supper, for you must need it," she said.

He followed her down a dark shrubbery. There were wild-flowers growing everywhere under the trees; he noticed a few late Hyacinths, and numberless Foxgloves.

"Have you come far?" she asked, turning and looking at him curiously.

"From London," he answered.

"Ah! I was only there once . . . to see the Queen's Jubilee. I lost my silver brooch there," she added as though talking to herself.

They turned an abrupt corner, which brought them in sight of the gardener's cottage. It was covered in creeper and Clematis, and looked rather damp, Wildred thought.

"Come in," she said, and led the way down an unlit passage.

In the kitchen his supper was waiting for him—some soup and an Irish stew. He sat down to please her, although he had no appetite.

There was a canary on the table, in a very small cage, that now and again sang a few notes to show that it was still awake. His hostess took some knitting, and drawing her chair up beside his began to talk.

"The family are still away," she said, "but Lady Appledore comes back tomorrow. Miss Iris is in the North with Fräulein, she has had measles, and has gone to Bury St. Edmunds to get well. You will be required to arrange the jardinières with plants tomorrow morning. Have you ever arranged before? Lady Appledore likes always blue or white flowers for her boudoir, and sometimes it's rather difficult. I don't know why there are so few blue flowers. She is a very eccentric lady, they say, and hard to please."

The girl paused a moment to count the stitches in the

sock she was making.

"Sometimes," she went on, "there are parties, and I get a glimpse of the swell folk through the trees. My! you should see the clothes they wear of an evening. I wonder they don't all catch cold. Miss Grantham, Lady Appledore's maid, once gave me, in return for a spray of Passion flowers, a little box of her ladyship's complexion. I have got it still, hidden away in an old boot, lest father should find it. He does not hold with them painted courtesans, he says, and their ways are not ours."

She paused for breath, and getting up, flung a cloth over the canary's cage, as the bird had commenced to sing.

"It is all very interesting what you tell me," Wildred said, as he finished his supper. "And now, please, where can I find your father?"

"Father is not to be disturbed," she said, beginning to clear away the table, "he is sitting up all night with a sick Orchid."

It must have been five o'clock the next morning when Wildred awoke. The sun was shining straight into his eyes, through the open window. From his bed he could see the tops of the fruit trees, clouded in pink blossom, already on the verge of falling.

"I am so glad it is fine," he murmured, "I couldn't have borne it to be wet my first morning, and the birds! Oh, listen!"

He sprang up and ran to the window. The room looked over an orchard bounded by mellow red brick walls, upon which Peach and Cherry trees were spread under voluminous-looking nets.

"The effect of the trailing white clouds, over the Cherry

blossom, and the long blue-green grass, is worthy of Daubigny," he told himself, as he proceeded to dress.

His toilet ended, he wondered what he should do.

"I suppose I had better go and look for Bartholomew, and introduce myself," and putting on a straw hat he went down into the garden.

"I shall probably find him in a greenhouse," Wildred thought, and sure enough in the first greenhouse he peeped into, he found an old man sleeping, his head carefully enveloped in a long grey shawl.

"It must be he," Wildred told himself, and clearing his throat to attract attention: "Good morning," he said.

The old man opened one eye, and stared at Wildred.

"Are you Sam's successor?" he enquired.

"I expect I am, at all events, I am the new gardener. I am sorry," he added, "to hear that you have an Orchid that is dying, I hope it will recover."

Old Bartholomew took the shawl from his head.

"The mauve Orchid is a little better this morning," he answered, "but she is low, very low. She passed as quiet a night as I could expect, and has closed her leaves now, thank God, and sleeps peaceful as a child. Speak softly, for she must not be disturbed. About one o'clock," he continued in a whisper, "I thought that she had gone . . . I lit my lanthorn and had a look at her. She had turned all black. Only a tinge of mauve round the heart told me that she still breathed."

"How perfectly terrible," murmured Wildred sympathetically. "But on such a lovely summer's morning, I am sure it cannot die; the song of the birds will give it dreams of the Jungle from whence it came. Think! poor flower, how it must pine for the wild nature that gave it birth. Perhaps on those endless afternoons when the sun scorched the Palm trees, and all the Jungle seemed shattered with heat, some green and silver snake may have coiled itself languorously

around it, and played with its black and purple leaves! And
on the white starry nights, when the Birds of Paradise, in the
tall Gum trees, cast their long shower plumes across the
moon, and the forest smelt sweet of Arum lilies . . . Ah!" he
broke off, "think of the difference of its present surround-
ings. A red pot on a shelf at Wiston!"

"And now will you kindly take this broom and sweep the
lawn before the house," old Bartholomew asked him, "for
her ladyship will be here today, and she does not like to see a
fallen leaf."

Wildred left old Bartholomew to his meditations, wondering what Lady Appledore could be like, if she disliked to
step on a fallen leaf.

"It probably reminds her that she is growing old," he told
himself, as he began to sweep.

But there was really no sign of a leaf anywhere, and it
seemed to him cruel to behead the Daisies.

It was the month of June, and the air was full of the fra-
grance of new-born flowers. Across the park the sun poured
down its gold on to the eager Buttercups, and encouraged
the drooping Cowslips. The birds were everywhere; they
flew down from the shadow of the trees, and opened their
grey wings to the warm morning, singing. Through the
branches of a tall Lime, the stable clock pointed to half past
six.

"It is frightfully early," Wildred told himself, "and I think I
shall lie down under this tree for a while, and smoke a
cigarette."

He stretched himself out on the grass, in the shadow of a
Lime, and watched the mist gathering in the park over the
woods. Overhead a wood-pigeon cooed deliciously, she
seemed to be brooding over some great happiness . . . so soft
was her voice. The long Elizabethan house was just visible to
him from where he lay. Every blind drawn down, it slept

solemnly on, heedless of the bright morning.

At seven o'clock Wildred saw the glass door, leading on to the terrace, open, and a housemaid appeared, broom in hand.

"I suppose I had better go and find out what flowers are wanted," he murmured, and crossed the lawn to the open door.

"Good morning," he said to the housemaid, who was standing on the doorstep, apparently dusting a Rose, "can you tell me where I shall find the butler?"

"Mr. Perfect is still in bed," replied the housemaid; "when the family are away, he rarely descends before eleven o'clock. You are the new gardener, I suppose?"

"I am," Wildred answered, "and I should be much obliged to you if you would show me what flowerpots I must fill."

"I shall be charmed," she murmured. "What is your name? Mine is Annie."

"And mine Wildred," he informed her. "I am sorry I have not a card with me."

"Oh do not trouble, besides it is not etiquette for an underservant to keep visiting cards. This is the drawing room. I will leave you to look round, I shall be back in a moment," and she darted away.

"What wonderful Dresden!" Wildred exclaimed, looking about him, "and this, I suppose must be the famous Flemish tapestry, and these the rock crystal wall lights that disappeared from the Vatican! Really Lady Appledore has the most perfect drawing room."

He wandered through the room admiring everything, now and again peeping at the title page of a book, or stooping down to look at a photograph.

He recognized, with a start, a portrait of his aunt, the Duchess of St. Andrews, standing on the grand piano, with her autograph "Queenie" written in hieroglyphics across her train, and on the same instrument his cousin, the beautiful Miss Clodah Forrester, the society actress, was seen in one of her most childlike parts.

"But what difference Mama does it make if I *do* marry Jim?" and her mother's reply, "But none, dear, none," Clodah had inscribed in copybook handwriting across the photo, and then in a corner, "Rôle of Ethel in *The Outcast.*"

"What a shock!" murmured Wildred, pressing his hand to his heart. "But Clodah, thank God, is in Hungary for the present, and the Duchess rarely comes further south than Newcastle, which she persists in always calling the Frontier. I remember the time she came down from Scotland, to stay with us in Park Street. After waiting dinner for her nearly two hours (mother in the meanwhile having retired for the night with *The Little Flowers of St. Francis* and a cornflour pudding), the dreadful peal we suddenly heard from the front door bell. "I hope it's not to say that the Prime Minister has had another relapse," father said, and just then the door flew open, and the Duchess burst in, and flung herself into poor mother's dressing room saying that she was without a night-gown or a maid, as she had lost them both crossing the Frontier. How long ago it all seems!" he said, looking at himself in a Queen Anne mirror, and rather admiring the dead-gold colour of his hair.

At that moment Annie returned. "If you would please to come this way," she said, "I will show you her ladyship's boudoir."

He followed her up a flight of stairs, into a charming room with bay windows, overlooking the park. The walls were hung mostly in old Dutch needlework, but here and there from a piece of mahogany paneling hung a rare print.

Alice, the third housemaid, was down on her knees polishing the parquet floor, but she stood up as they entered, and came forward to be introduced.

"This room has never been photographed for the papers like the rest of the house," she said by way of conversation, "it is her ladyship's little holy-of-holies. Please be careful when you are putting pots in the Chinese jardinières not to chip them, for they are museum pieces."

On the staircase Annie pointed out a faded blue and gold box, studded with nails.

"It is always filled with small Almond trees," she said, "her ladyship likes it done with nothing else. It was once part of the marriage equipment of Miss Isabella d'Este, a young lady of the Italian Renaissance."

"Her husband was a Podesta," called out Alice over the landing, "which, Mr. Perfect says, means the same thing as a Doge."

❧

As he was carrying a basket of peaches and white roses towards the house, for the dinner table, he came suddenly across Lady Appledore.

She had evidently only just arrived, for she wore a long grey dust cloak, and a large black hat, bedecked with ostrich feathers, that looked very much like London. She was seated in a basket chair, talking to her dogs. A foreign-looking little woman, in a tailor-made gown, stood beside her, fanning herself with a magnolia leaf.

"Probably Mademoiselle Doucet, the companion," thought Wildred, who had heard of her from the gardener's daughter.

He touched his cap to Lady Appledore as he passed, and murmured "good evening," but she did not seem to notice him, for she went on playing with her dogs.

As he returned with the empty basket, however, she glanced up and called him.

"How is the Orchid?" she enquired.

"Better, I believe, your ladyship, but I have not yet seen it," Wildred answered.

"You are Wildred, the new gardener, are you not? and you have been three years with Sir George Liss? When you were at Holton, did you have much experience in arranging herbaceous borders? and do you, I wonder, grasp the meaning of colour, which in a gardener, I maintain, is almost as important as keeping early hours, and not being tempted into the public house?"

"I used to have the reputation of always wearing the most harmonious ties, your ladyship," he answered humbly.

She raised her eyebrows. "Really. I am not interested. But do you realise that Paeonies and Lobelia are not suitable together? that flowers can make the most undesirable marriages, just as—" she raised her large dark eyes to his, and studied his face for the first time.

His curly dim-gold hair, the delicate skin, the beautifully shaped mouth and hands, and his wide grey eyes made her forget what she was saying.

"Have I never seen you before?" she asked, "but I suppose I must have noticed you at Holton, when I was staying last Easter with Sir George."

The dressing gong sounded from the house just then, and she rose to go.

Wildred looked at her in amazement. "She is perfectly lovely," he told himself, "I have never seen anybody quite so beautiful."

"I shall want you to bring me a large basket of flowers in the morning," she said, "choice ones, as they are for decorating the summerhouse of Apollo."

"Certainly," he replied, "and I think the idea is delightful. Good night, your ladyship."

She looked at him in astonishment.

"Good night, Wildred," she said, and went into the house.

He stood for a moment looking after her, tingling with delight. She had called him Wildred!

The bats flew past him, circling wildly, almost brushing him with their wings; from every window lamps showed, shrouded by soft-coloured shades. Oh! if he were in Italy, now he would seize a guitar and sing.

"You fool," he told himself, "gardeners are always called by their Christian names." But how wonderfully she had said it. Wildred. Wildred!

He wandered away from the house, and went towards the park. The long grass was drenched with dew; away beyond the woods the sun was almost out of sight, only on the topmost boughs of the tall Elm trees lingered a ray of gold. He wandered on, attracted in the distance by the gleam of water.

That Greek-looking temple through the trees must be Apollo's summerhouse.

He drew near.

Emerging from between the delicate marble columns of the temple, as though about to plunge himself into the lake, stood a slim Apollo, his head bent a little forward, peering down at his own white form in the trembling water.

"He looks ever so much more like Narcissus than Apollo," said Wildred, and seating himself on the river bank he recited to the first moonbeam that touched the lake, a poem of Verlaine.

❧

The next morning, the paper said, was the hottest day of the year.

"And to think that I must water the herbaceous borders," he said; "how much pleasanter it would be to sit in the orchard with a book!"

He was dressed in an old cricket blazer, and a soft silk shirt open at the neck, his Panama hat well turned down over the eyes.

"It is really delicious to be able to wear what one likes," he murmured, "supposing I were in London now, I should be wearing stays and a frock coat. Ugh! How ripe and fresh those peaches look," he went on admiringly, "I simply cannot resist them. That ripe, pink-looking peach is, I am sure, the mother of all those little green ones, it would be cruel to take *her*. But these!!" He filled both pockets of his blazer with fruit, and then scrambled up into a beech tree to enjoy it.

The sunlight shining through the leaves was so beautiful that it seemed to him that each leaf must be an emerald, and the song of a thrush, just on a bough above, lulled him to entrancing drowsiness.

In all probability he must have fallen asleep, for presently he became conscious that someone was calling him as though from a great distance. He opened his eyes. "Yes, what is it?" he murmured.

On the path below stood Lady Appledore, looking up at him in amazement.

"What are you doing up there?" she enquired.

"I felt a little languid," he explained, "the morning is so hot."

"Languid! *Languid!* I never heard of such a thing, I cannot possibly allow you to feel languid whilst my roses perish for water."

He clambered from his branch, sending down a shower of peach stones, that fell at Lady Appledore's feet.

"You are fond of peaches, I see," she remarked. "Do you think that a languid gardener, who makes siestas in trees, and is fond of peaches, is quite the person I want?"

"I am indeed sorry, your ladyship," Wildred murmured,

and he looked so handsome in his garden get-up that Lady Appledore said nothing more.

"I hadn't the heart to send him away," she told Mademoiselle Doucet at lunch, "he has the most beautiful face I have ever seen."

❦

That night it rained. How close! how intimate it sounded, pattering down on the thirsty leaves outside!

His room was so full of shadows that he could not see the time. He could just distinguish the dark outline of the trees in the orchard below his window; he had thought that in the country there was always a moon!

"I am afraid all this damp will give the nightingales sore throats," he told himself, "and how tiresome that I should have wasted my day in watering Roses when nature herself was only waiting for the opportunity. There is one comfort, I shall have an idle day tomorrow," and he meditated what books he should read. "Ronsard in the morning would be charming, and D'Annunzio in the afternoon," he decided as he fell asleep.

He dreamt of peach stones, and a lady with a lace parasol, whose face he could not see.

He awoke with a start, hearing the sound of gravel thrown against his windowpane.

Old Bartholomew was standing below in the wet.

"Are you dreaming that you was your own master, and would you like your breakfast sent up to you on a tray?" he enquired. "You may not be aware that it has gone eight."

"Bother the old man!" exclaimed Wildred, as he dressed. "I thought I was to have had a quiet morning to myself, and just look at the rain!"

He was told by old Bartholomew when he went downstairs, that it was the day appointed for changing the plants in the house.

Really it was a nuisance to have to trundle palm trees through the wet, but there was no help for it so it seemed.

He found Mademoiselle Doucet in the morning room, having breakfast, when he entered.

"Good morning," she remarked, "what an unpleasant day!"

"It is indeed, Mademoiselle, but it will cool the air."

She continued her breakfast, glancing now and then at a letter by her side.

"Ah, non pas comme ça!" she exclaimed suddenly looking up.

He was endeavouring to squeeze a red Camellia tree into the same jardinière as some Maiden Hair ferns, that seemed most unwilling to yield the desired inch.

"Pas comme ça?" he asked, "mais alors que voulez vous que je fasse?"

She looked at him in amazement.

"You speak French?" she demanded.

"Yes, Mademoiselle, only a little."

"Comment donc! but it is extraordinary."

"How extraordinary?"

"Mais, je ne sais pas, but as a rule, gardeners . . ."

"But, Mademoiselle, I have not *always* been a gardener."

"No?"

How frightfully imprudent of him, he must take care.

"No," he remarked smilingly, "I was once over in Paris—in business there, I was a . . . a . . . an assistant in a hair-dresser's shop! Chez Rubens, you know, in the rue de la Paix."

"Mon Dieu!" gasped Mademoiselle Doucet, "then perhaps sometimes you could arrange my hair for me, it is so very troublesome. Ah! what happiness to find a coiffeur from

chez Rubens dans un lieu si sauvage, and how delighted
Lady Appledore will be!"

૨

"My dear, he is no such thing," Lady Appledore told her,
"and even if he were, I should never dream of allowing him
to do my hair."

They were driving into Minster-le-Hope to meet a nest of
plover's eggs that were coming down from town by rail.

"How much less fussy it is to meet a plover's nest than a
friend," Lady Appledore reflected.

"Good afternoon," she called to the Vicar, who flew past
on his bicycle as though he were trying to circumvent the
Devil.

"What a glorious day, dear lady," he called out to her, "I
am hastening to the station to meet my wife."

"Malheureux!" Mademoiselle Doucet murmured sympathetically, "but do let us stop at the Post Office and get the
letters," she suggested, "it's my poor mother's day for
writing."

"She writes very often to you," Lady Appledore remarked
dryly. "Does she still live at Versailles?"

"Yes, in the Cour la Reine, but oh do look at that field of
Buttercups, did you ever see anything quite so golden, on
dirait un morceau de . . . de . . ."

"Yes! here's the post," exclaimed Lady Appledore.

"Are there any letters?" she enquired.

The woman handed them to her. "Will you take the
servants' letters also?" she asked.

"Yes, we may as well, and it will save your son a walk."

The postmistress beamed on Lady Appledore.

"Such a hot day! What dusty roads! and how unfortunate
that Minster-le-Hope wasn't nearer the sea!" She ran from

subject to subject without pausing to breathe. "Come and look at my Phloxes," she invited, "they are the finest in all the village. Most of the neighbours only find time for growing Candytuft, but I thinks no country garden should be without a bit of Sweet William, and a Colombine or two."

As they passed down the village street, a face flew to every window, to see the beautiful lady and the prancing horses, but Lady Appledore was feeling decidedly bored. There were no letters of any interest, and the gaping children, rolling in the dust, failed just then to appeal to her instinct of the picturesque.

"But who are all the letters for?" enquired Mademoiselle Doucet with curiosity.

Lady Appledore sorted them out. "One for Mrs. Gwatkin, and all the rest, yes! every one of them! are for the new gardener."

"Would it be very wrong, I wonder, to open one, and see who it was from," murmured Mademoiselle Doucet.

"My dear!" exclaimed Lady Appledore horrified, "how could you think of such a thing! This one," she went on, holding a long lilac-tinted envelope up to the sun, "is from the Duchess of St. Andrews, I know the handwriting. But why will she always write on such thick paper? It has been forwarded on from the Pall Mall Club. Surely, *surely,* the man cannot be a member of the Pall Mall Club?"

Mademoiselle Doucet shivered. "I have a presentiment that he may be a burglar, or an Anarchist," she said. "Oh! dear Lady Appledore, I shall never dare go to sleep tonight, and the key in my bedroom door won't turn."

"I will have the lock arranged immediately," Lady Appledore assured her, "but do not be nervous, dear Mademoiselle Doucet, for I feel convinced that the only thing that may be destroyed through this man's presence are my flowers."

"We are in God's hands," Mademoiselle Doucet said

piously, as the carriage turned into the drive, "and oh look!" she suddenly screamed, shielding herself behind her parasol, "he is standing there hiding behind a tree, I believe he is taking aim at me with a pistol, and means to fire."

"Don't be so absurd," Lady Appledore said, "and do try and control your mind."

"Wildred," she called to him, "here are letters for you, come and take them."

He came forward, trying to hide a book behind his back.

Mademoiselle Doucet nearly fainted. "I see the gleam of the trigger," she murmured, and closing her eyes waited for the explosion.

"Thank you, your ladyship," Wildred answered, taking the letters with a slight bow.

"What are you holding behind your back so carefully?" Lady Appledore asked him.

"This," said Wildred, looking horribly guilty, and holding up a beautifully bound volume.

"May I see?"

He handed it to her.

She looked at him puzzled. "You read Omar Khayyám, and what a lovely edition! I am afraid you are very extravagant, but better spend your money so than in the public house."

"And now home," she said to the coachman.

~

The next day was Sunday.

Dressed all in white, with a large shady hat, garlanded with blue Hortensias, Lady Appledore sat under a lime tree reading.

Her book was a study on the Architecture of Valladolid Cathedral. Lady Appledore loved remote books, the more distant the subject to her everyday life, the more she was charmed.

Novels about Society bored her, although she was fond of reading plays, but a treatise on industries that would have no interest to her in real life, delighted her in books.

Thus, a short essay on the Manufcture of Strawberry-punnets thrilled her to enthusiasm. "It soothed me, it lulled me like nothing else," she had told a royal lady, who was complaining of feeling nervous at night.

"It is so delicious to know something about the Moors," she murmured, "they *must* have been dears."

The quiet thread of her thoughts was rudely broken upon by Grantham, her maid, who appeared just then with a parasol and a prayer-book.

"Your ladyship will be late for Church," she remarked, "it is eleven o'clock already."

Wildred too had gone into Minster-le-Hope for the morning service.

It was such a delightful old Church, with quaint carved monuments fixed into niches in the wall, and from where Wildred sat he could see the quiet churchyard bathed in full sunshine, and he noticed the simple tomb of Oliver Cromwell's mother, over which a rambling red rose tree cast its flowers.

He sang so well that several people turned to see who was the owner of the warm rich voice, and after the service the Vicar called him aside and asked him to join the choir.

Some of the servants from Wiston were waiting outside in the porch.

"You will have to come and sing to us one evening," Mr. Perfect the butler graciously invited him. "Arthur, the second footman, plays the banjo, and Violet, the kitchen-maid, is a skilful amateur of the concertina, and when her ladyship is out driving, and all the doors are closed, Squire, the pantry boy, plays us selections on the bassoon."

Annie and Alice asked him if he were fond of musical comedy, but Mrs. Gwatkin, the cook, who had just gone over to the Plymouth Brethren, did not think the subject quite fitted to Sunday, and changed the conversation by alluding to the heat.

"How unpleasant to be a cow!" she said, pointing with her parasol towards the park. "Poor things! I wonder they don't get sunstroke with no hats on their heads but their horns."

Mr. Perfect agreed. "But I am no friend to cows," he said, "they are such licentious animals. Things as has no tables of kindred and affinity are not to be respected."

"I wish," said Lady Appledore to Mademoiselle Doucet, as they passed the servants, "that Perfect would not wear poor Appledore's clothes, although I know he gave them to him; they do *so* get on my nerves."

⁂

But it is always the unexpected that happens, and one morning as Wildred was busy digging up cabbages, he was startled to hear a familiar voice behind him.

"My dear Wildred, what on earth are you doing? I had no idea that you were one of the house party, I never noticed you at dinner last night."

He turned round, and to his horror beheld the Duchess of St. Andrews.

"Aunt Queenie!" he gasped, and let his spade fall to the ground with a clatter.

"You do not seem quite yourself," she remarked, "but why these Tolstoi habits?" and she pointed to the spade.

"My dear Aunt, you had best be told at once," he said, "be seated, and prepare yourself for a great shock"; and digging the blade of his spade deep into the soil, he offered her the handle for a chair. "Be as comfortable as possible," he hospitably recommended her, "and remember not to lean back."

The Duchess opened her parasol. "I shall have freckles this evening if I remain here long," she complained, "so be as quick as you can."

"Then, dear Aunt, I am Lady Appledore's gardener."

The Duchess was overcome. "Oh my spoilt child, that it should have come to this!" she screamed, "that a nephew of mine . . ." Words failed her. She sought vainly to articulate with her garden gauntlets, the Nasturtiums in her hat shook convulsively, although there was no wind to stir them.

"I cannot see, Aunt, what difference it makes to you."

"Oh! what would your poor-dear-misguided-ambitious mother say now, could she behold you weeding cabbages?" she cried.

"She would be the last to blame me. But, dear Aunt, I wish to remain on here, and do not want Lady Appledore to know who I am. Be so good as to say nothing about it."

The Duchess looked at him in astonishment.

"You *wish* to remain here as her gardener?"

"Certainly. Do you know I have never been so happy before. Of course, I dare say I shall give gardening up during the winter, when the weather changes, but these long summer days spent among flowers and fruit charm me beyond words. You have no idea how peaceful my life has been since I arrived at Wiston. No responsibility, nothing to worry about, and all around the good beautiful country, the fresh wildflowers, the free birds, and my friends the trees. Oh, dear Aunt Queenie, do not spoil my happiness."

"My dearest child, far from it. I am beginning now to think you merely eccentric, and I will even encourage you in your new profession, by presenting you with a complete set of garden tools of your own."

"My dear, generous Aunt!"

"But tell me," she went on, "aren't you a little wee bit in love with Clarida Appledore?"

"Well, then, yes I am," he admitted, "and it's just the case of Ruy Blas all over again!"

"I hope not, and I would do my best to help you, but you must see that as long as you are her gardener, it is improper even to think of a wedding. However, come and have tea with me this afternoon, everybody is going to a garden party, so I shall be all alone, and we can talk over everything then."

"Thanks, Aunt, but you forget the servants. What would Perfect say if he saw us having tea together?"

"Well then, I will tell him to have tea in the Rose Garden. Bring your spade with you, and if anyone comes in sight you can begin to dig. Au revoir."

❦

"I spent the morning in the garden," the Duchess said at lunch. "What wonderful Roses you have this year, dear, and what a handsome gardener! Where did you get him from?"

"I noticed the man from my bedroom window," said old Lady Gloria Townley, "I thought what a perfect footman!"

"Mademoiselle Doucet believes he is an Anarchist," said Lady Appledore, "she will not go out on the terrace after twilight, for fear he should murder her."

"An Anarchist! my nephew an Anarchist! my dear Clarida, what next?"

The Duchess was furious.

"Your nephew, Duchess? What *do* you mean?"

"Oh! how stupid of me to have told you, he doesn't wish it known, but I couldn't hear one of my own blood spoken of as an Anarchist without protesting. However, dear, he *is* my

nephew—poor Goda's boy—you know they lost all their
money in that horrid coal mine. Still, I believe, Wildred will
have about £800 a year, when all the claims are settled, and
if he is careful he should be able to manage on that, he is
only doing gardening temporarily."

"This is indeed an interesting young man," exclaimed the
Bishop of Margate, who was one of the party. "I must try and
interview him after lunch for my parochial magazine."

"We must ask him in to dine with us this evening," Lady
Appledore said. "Oh! I am so delighted, Duchess, that he
is your nephew, I felt all along that he was no *ordinary*
gardener."

"I fell quite in love with him from the bathroom window,"
Lady Gloria exclaimed. And then, turning to the Bishop, she
suddenly remarked apropos of nothing, "Oh the tragedy,
Bishop, to be called Gloria when one is over sixty!" and she
shook her grey curls, and looked away through the open
French window, her blue eyes fixed dreamily on the white
Peacocks, that stood upon the terrace spreading their tails
to the sun.

The Bishop, whose esprit was never very bright after
lunch, was mercifully saved making a gallant repartee by
Perfect, who tactfully asked him whether he would take
Kümmel or Curaçao.

❦

Although the stable clock had struck eleven, the night was
so bright that he could see to pack without a lamp. The ugly
white case stood in the centre of a patch of moonlight, his
music and books scattered all around over the uncarpeted
floor.

Yes, he was going. How could he stay now that all was
known? Had not the Bishop of Margate tried to interview

him that afternoon as he was gathering melons for a water ice, and had not Lady Appledore asked him to dinner and music afterwards? Oh! he felt that he would like to strangle the Duchess for her indiscretion.

Tomorrow night he would be back in London again. He had heard from his solicitor that there would be about £800 a year, saved for him out of the débris, but what a shame it was that he could not go on earning Lady Appledore's eighteen-shillings-and-sixpence a week until the end of the summer. He had been so happy at Wiston. He had never been so happy before.

He leaned his arm down on the windowsill, and gazed up at the night.

The sky was glorious with stars, and the moon hung low over the orchard, like a golden apricot on the verge of falling.

The long grass was alight with glowworms, thousands and thousands of them, so that they appeared to be the reflections of the stars in a still green lake. Hidden amongst the yellow tassels of the Laburnum flower, a bird was telling of all the marvels it had seen across the seas.

"As far as I can understand," said Wildred, listening, "she spent last winter in Egypt, with her family; and her youngest daughter, who is very delicate, married a Martin there, and is living in the utmost warmth and comfort in a charming Pyramid, just outside Cairo. This year, she says, she is going to Spain, she longs to visit the Alhambra, and if the Moon will grant her strength of wings, she hopes to fly home by Persia, as she has an invitation to pass a weekend in the Shah's garden: and now," said Wildred, "I can no longer understand what she says, but I think she must be doing a serenade by Chaminade."

The stable clock chimed midnight.

"Hullo! I must get on with my packing," he murmured,

"but all the same it is not *really* extraordinary that I should be a wee bit in love with Lady Appledore, when the very tiniest bird in the garden has got its mate."

৺

Lady Appledore could not sleep.

She had tried poetry, bromide, and a biographical history of higher Philosophy, and she was still awake.

"It is most extraordinary!" she murmured. "I suppose it must be the heat."

She opened her window, and sat there admiring the beauty of the park at night. "How wonderful the trees were, and the blue chain of hills beyond, how peaceful!"

"I can so well understand why such numbers of the Saints flew to the hills," she told herself, "I should do exactly the same."

The scent of flowers rose up from underneath her window —Mignonette, Jasmine, Roses.

"It's no use," she exclaimed at last, "I cannot pretend any longer I do not know what's the matter. I love him."

A peacock floated down from the Cedar tree before the house, and stretched its wings to the first bar of silver light that showed above the woods.

Lady Appledore closed her window.

"You silly woman," she said to her mirror, "you will look so plain in the morning after this sleepless night, and it serves you right for being so foolish. He is going away today and doesn't care that for you!"

She took the long pearl earrings from her ears, and deposed them for the night on the vellum cover of a Thomas à Kempis.

"Oh! I cannot help it," she murmured, beginning to sob, "and I must be natural for once, and as there's no one to see me, it doesn't much matter."

And spreading herself comfortably on a sofa she indulged in a delicious cry.

꒰꒱

At eight o'clock next morning, when Grantham knocked at Lady Appledore's bedroom door with her cup of chocolate, she was surprised to receive no answer, and still more so when, on entering the room, she did not find her mistress.

"What can have happened?" Grantham wondered, and noticing that the bed had not been slept in, she immediately began to investigate.

"The case looks almost parallel to that of my last poor mistress," she murmured, "where can her ladyship have gone? The nearest creature of prepossessing appearance lives quite half-an-hour's carriage drive away from here, and it would take over three-quarters of an hour to go on foot, and then by taking all the short cuts."

She picked up a paperbound French novel, and disapproved of the cover. *L'Amour chez les Turques,* she read.

"I hope her ladyship will not think of going so far as Turkey, the thoughts of a Harem make my blood freeze; and besides, no nice maid likes going further than Paris. When I went to Biarritz last year, and got out at Bayonne by mistake, I thought I should have died."

She met Alice on the staircase sweeping.

"Have you seen her ladyship?" she enquired.

"Yes, she has gone riding, she passed me half an hour ago, she told me to say she would like breakfast at ten."

"You are sure she has not been gone more than half an hour?"

"Quite."

Grantham felt disappointed. Life was so dull in the country,

she had hoped that it might have been something a little
more exciting.

༜

Wildred stood on the platform waiting for the train. It was
already signaled, but there were five minutes yet before it
would start.

The village of Minster-le-Hope appeared over the low
white palings of the station, faint and misty as a crayon drawing, in the early morning air.

The grey church tower seemed to exhort the trees about
it to grow higher, higher, and the sky above was of such a
delicate shade of blue, that it looked as if it had been
powdered all over with poudre de riz.

The sound of a horse cantering swiftly broke the silence.

Through the gold broom he caught sight of a woman on
horseback.

Could it be? Yes! it was Lady Appledore.

He had never seen her on horseback before. She looked
bewitching in her close-fitting habit, and how unusual was
the violet pom-pom in her hat!

He ran to meet her.

"Good morning," he said, "I am sorry, but I was running
away with the key of the Orchid-house on my watch chain,
what luck that I should meet you."

She smiled at him as she took it.

"I wanted to say good-bye to you," she said. "I wanted to
tell you that . . . that I think it was a very sweet idea of yours
to be a gardener! and I hope that we shall often meet again in
London. Will you come and see me sometimes in Berkeley
Square? You will always be welcome."

She held out her hand to him.

He took it and kissed it.

"My dear lady," he said, "I am sorry to have to leave you. I have been so happy at Wiston, I am afraid I shall never be as happy again, unless"—he broke off—"Oh promise to write and tell me all about the herbaceous borders, and whether old Bartholomew succeeds in inventing a grey Geranium! You do not know how much all your news will interest me."

The train was in sight, coming round the bend of the line.

"Good-bye," she said. "Good-bye, Mr. Forrester."

"You used to call me Wildred," he reminded her.

"Ah! that was yesterday—before I knew."

She kissed her hand to him as the train steamed out of Minster Station, and he waved his hat back to her from his third-class carriage.

She remained waving till the train was lost from view.

"Well I never! no! certainly I never did!" exclaimed the station master.

❧

A year later, on a hot June afternoon, as Mrs. Watson the Vicar's wife was returning from her devotions, she happened to meet Mrs. Massey, the new châtelaine of Cheapthorpe Priory.

Mrs. Massey was the rich wife of a Bond Street jeweller.

"Her earrings are almost more trying to the eyes than the sun," was Mrs. Watson's reflection as she opened her parasol.

"Good morning," Mrs. Massey said, "am I late for Church?"

She was a small woman, faultlessly dressed in a linen gown by Worth, her pyramid of bright red hair was an exact match of the Water Naiad's in Henner's picture at the Luxembourg.

"Yes, service is over," Mrs. Watson told her. "Today is the festival of St. Enias."

"Was not St. Enias before his conversion the husband of an Italian girl who danced the Tarantella?" asked Mrs. Massey, who loved gossip, "or am I thinking of somebody else?"

As Mrs. Watson had never heard of the Tarantella she spoke of the Vicar's health.

"He is frightfully overworked," she complained, "and in our small parish, you will hardly credit it, there are no fewer than three widowed peeresses, and a wounded general."

"A wounded general!" exclaimed Mrs. Massey, "how pathetic!"

"He lives in the big white house you can see through the trees. They never found the bullet."

"Poor lingering man! But do you think, Mrs. Watson, that he would care to come to tea, if I wrote a nice little note and asked him?"

"My dear, he never leaves his couch," Mrs. Watson informed her. "The Vicar sometimes goes and reads to him, but he does not seem to listen, just goes on playing with his toy soldiers, exterminating Dervishes that his housekeeper buys for him in boxes in the village."

"I will send him a case of real good ones from the Stores," said Mrs. Massey, much moved, "but tell me, Mrs. Watson, who lives in that red Victorian-looking house?"

"It's Elizabethan," Mrs. Watson informed her, "and belongs to Mrs. Wildred Forrester. You must have heard of her as Lady Appledore. Poor Lord Appledore! such a good man! such a staunch Protestant! so different from his frivolous wife! Her second marriage was disgraceful, the Vicar refused to marry them, so they had to go to Knightsbridge. Why, my dear Mrs. Massey, I have *seen* Mr. Forrester come round to the Vicarage back door with a basket of Seakale! Of course when she married him she tried to get people to believe he was well connected. Said he was a nephew of the

Duchess of St. Andrews, and a cousin of *the* Forresters. But whatever the relationship *may* have been, I feel thoroughly convinced that it has not been properly renewed since the days of Noah."

Mrs. Massey looked bewildered. "But who was her husband?" she enquired.

"You may well ask; and you will scarcely believe me when I tell you that Lady Appledore married her gardener!"

Mrs. Massey stood still, and clutched at Mrs. Watson's arm for support.

"I never heard of such a mésalliance," she gasped.

Appendix

The Wind & the Roses
(To be set to music)

Poor pale Pierrot, through the dark boughs peering
In the purple gloaming of a summer's evening—
Oh! his heart is bleeding, can't you hear him sobbing?
Or is it the wind that's sighing amongst the yellow roses?

Hush! . . . .

'Tis the wind that's sighing amongst the yellow roses.

Wrapped in bluest shadow, poor Pierrot hiding
Sees the faithless Pierrette for her lover waiting
She sits by a fountain in an Italian garden
And her tiny hands are full of scarlet tulips.

'Neath the dark boughs Pierrot, for the moon is waiting.
He can see the sky like the blue sea dreaming
And a great gold cloud like a net is gleaming
an amber lure for silver fishes—

Then near at hand a voice starts singing,
And a harp like a soul in love sounds throbbing
through the turquoise air—
And midst the boughs poor Pierrot spying, sees Colombine
    draw near.

151

Tall Colombine through the waving roses
that cling about him like pale faces
Crushes beneath his satin slippers
the red oleanders, and the sleeping violets—

Pierrette, smiling at her mirror, sees her lover's form reflected
All amongst the cloud-white roses—
Then letting fall her scarlet tulips, she trips amongst the bleeding
    fuschias
and embraces Colombine with many kisses—

Poor pale Pierrot, through the dark boughs peering
Hears the kisses of his own dear loved one
and his heart now sore, & quite, quite broken
He stabs himself with a silver dagger—

Far away in the country dreary
The blue hills, 'neath the round moon weary
Seem lost in thought—

Hush! . . .

On a green bough bending
A nightingale is sobbing
out a tale of love—

See! the grey light dawning
Pierrette has found Pierrot lying
With a knife in his heart.

Hush! . . . . is she crying . . . . ?

No . . . . 'Tis only the wind that's sighing
amongst the yellow roses.

An Early Flemish Painter

At the *Exposition de la Toison d'Or,* at Bruges, there is a wonderful portrait of Charles Quint. The face, long and slightly upturned, appears like a wax mask chiseled to rare distinction against its sombre setting. The eyes, full of thought, seem a little weary; the lips, parted, inhale, one would say, some sweet perfume; the hair, descending low upon the neck, falls from beneath the brim of a black velvet hat, aslant, encrusted with pearls, whilst on a round jewel one reads the inscription: *Sancta Maria, ora pro nobis.* The potrait is attributed to Jean Gossart. Jean Gossart was born at Maubeuge in Hainaut, between 1470-1475. Little is known of his early youth: it would seem that in his sixteenth year he came to Bruges, and became a pupil of Memling. How long he stayed with Memling is uncertain, but Memling died about 1495, and in the year 1503 we hear of one Jasmyn Mabuise, a painter, residing in Antwerp.

Were Jasmyn Mabuise and Jean of Maubeuge identical? It seems probable, for Jean Gossart is referred to variously in the registers of the time as Jenni Gossart, Jehannin Mabuze, or, again, Johannes Malbodius, taking his surname from the town in which he was born. If Jasmyn Mabuise and Jean Gossart are the same, he must certainly, whilst in Antwerp, have studied directly under Quentin Metsys, whose influence is apparent in his early work. Till the age of thirty Jean remained in Flanders, imitating, with that personal

note entirely his, such masters as Memling, Van Eyck, Quentin
Metsys, and Roger Van der Weyden. It was in the summer of 1508
that Gossart first met Philippe de Burgogne. The duke invited him
to his court, and soon afterwards, in the October of the same year,
Gossart set out for Rome in the duke's suite, a brilliant company
that included the Cardinal of Saint Croix, bound on a diplomatic
mission to Pope Julius II.

The Renaissance in Italy was then in full flower, and Gossart, his
mind rigid with Gothic influence, seems to have been over-
whelmed by this new beauty that so suddenly came upon him.
The spirit of a new ideal awoke in Jean's soul. It was in Italy for
the first time that he beheld Botticelli, and *The Last Supper* of
Leonardo da Vinci, then in its first freshness, was not yet ten years
old. In this same year Michael Angelo finished his frescoes for
the roof of the Sistine Chapel, and Ariosto was busy weaving his
Orlando. Can it be wondered at that, on Gossart's return to
Flanders, the recollection of this gay wealth of colour should
haunt his fancy, and from onwards an indecision crept into his
work, the influence of Italy alluring him from those sterner
schools of the North, which, however, were too deeply imbued
in him to entirely forget?

And his work becomes an experiment. The strong blues and
reds that hitherto he had massed together in incomparable
richness, now change to delicate greens and fragile shades of
turquoise. He begins to drape his figures in the Italian style,
making use lavishly of pearls and precious stones, of flowers, and
birds of brilliant plumage, and amidst this splendour he sets
anxious-looking Flemish Madonnas, a little bewildered, perhaps,
at this new luxury. It was after Gossart's return from Italy that
Charles Quint commissioned him to paint his sister, the Princess
Eleanor of Austria; what more likely, then, that Charles himself
should sit to Gossart for a portrait?

It would seem that about this time Charles Quint made a pro-
longed visit at the Flemish Court, and a delightful anecdote relates
how the duke, wishing to display his munificence, presented his
favourite painter, philosopher, and historian, each with a robe of

white damask embroidered with golden sprays of flowers. The evening before Charles arrived, Gossart pledged and lost his robe at dice. Repairing swiftly to his house, Jean spent the rest of that night and the next day painting a paper robe for himself so exquisitely with flowers, that at the banquet given in Charles's honour, the King exclaimed at it, saying that it surpassed anything in beauty that he ever wished to see! One thing more is known of the life of Gossart, his friendship with the painter Lucas de Leyden. Together, these two journeyed through Flanders, entertaining magnificently all the artists of the towns at which they stopped. It was at one of these feasts that Lucas was poisoned. Gossart, whose health seems to have suffered from these orgies, disappears soon after, and is lost amidst the shadows of the Middle Ages; it is supposed that he died in the year 1533.

Some of his most beautiful pictures are in England. *The Man with the Rosary* is in the National Gallery, *Adam and Eve* at Hampton Court, *The Adoration of the Magi* at Castle Howard. In the Scottish National Portrait Gallery at Edinburgh he is represented by a beautiful portrait of a lady, and there is a wondrous portrait of Jean Carondelet in the Louvre. His work, at once imitative and personal, wavers continually between the influences of the Flemish School and the Italian Renaissance. Like a man unable to decide whether he shall turn to the right or the left, he tries to make a compromise, a blending of both. The effect is curious.

Textual Notes

The pieces collected in this volume constitute Ronald Firbank's literary apprenticeship, a five-year period (1903–8) during which he worked through a variety of styles, genres, and voices, both imitating and subverting the literary models of his day. Written between the ages of seventeen and twenty-two, they are, properly speaking, his juvenilia, and are not to be judged by the standards of his mature work. All the seeds of the later work, however, were planted in this early work, and it is instructive and entertaining to observe Firbank as he tends his literary garden.

Of the seventeen pieces collected here, only eight were published in Firbank's lifetime. Writing to American novelist Carl Van Vechten in 1925 (a year before his death), Firbank reports "I have found lately a number of my early writings preserved by my mother & among her papers. . . . However I think it a mistake to publish at random, & am only so glad I had the tact as a child not to rush headlong into print." He went through these writings and marked most of them "Not to be published" (or "Not to publish"), relenting only in the case of "Lady Appledore's Mésalliance" to wonder "? Revise considerably in places—If—." Despite Firbank's injunction, all but four of his early stories eventually found their way into print—mostly in limited editions published in the 1960s and 1970s—and those four now join the rest in this first complete collection.

After deciding on the contents (I've excluded only fragments and rough drafts), the next step was to establish a chronological order so that Firbank's literary development could be followed.

Here I relied almost completely on the researches of the late Miriam J. Benkovitz. In her biography, her bibliography, and in her introductions to the limited editions of some of these pieces, Benkovitz provides all the known details of Firbank's life and offers the most plausible chronology for his work. (A much livelier biography has been written by Brigid Brophy, but she has little to say on this matter; a new biography is reportedly being written by Julian Bezel.) Chronological particulars will be given in the individual notes below.

Editing the stories presented the greatest difficulty. Even in his published texts Firbank is erratic and idiosyncratic in his spelling and punctuation, and in his unpublished writings more so. Resisting the temptation to standardize everything, I decided to let Firbank have his way as often as possible, however, and confined myself to following the instructions he gave one of his typists: "Keep punc. & cap. letters. Correct spell only." Even there, it would have been pedantic to correct his "*the Walkuries*" to *Die Walküre* or his "Mona Liza" to Mona Lisa, or to assume that his Prince Borris would have probably spelled his name Boris; only more egregious errors, like "*Salommé*" for Strauss's *Salome,* have been corrected. Firbank's old-fashioned punctuation remains, as does his British spelling, but I have used American-style double quotes to indicate dialogue (as Firbank himself did). A few modernizations have been made (such as "tonight" for "to-night"), unnecessary hyphens deleted, and the use of italics regularized for all book titles, newspapers, operas, and so on. I've aimed for a certain consistency throughout, but have not let consistency become a hobgoblin. A few problematic readings are given in the notes below, but this collection is intended to be a trade edition of Firbank's stories, not a scholarly one. Firbank scholars—if such creatures still exist; according to the annual *MLA Bibliography,* hardly a word has been written on Firbank in a decade—will want to consult the originals.

I want to thank Firbank collector Maurice B. Cloud for loaning materials and making suggestions; Scott Hercher (formerly of Swann Galleries) and Tom Goldwasser (of Serendipity Books) for helping me to track down the owner of the typescripts of "The Legend of Saint Gabrielle" and "Her Dearest Friend," and Barry Humphries for sending me copies; Mary M. Huth of Rush Rhees Library (University of Rochester) for photocopies of "True Love" and "The Singing Bird & the Moon"; Clifford S. Mead of Kerr Library (Oregon State University) for locating a copy of "Souvenir d'Automne"; Mrs. Beatrix Hammarling for permission to use her late husband Edgell Rickword's English translations of Firbank's French prose poems; and especially Colonel Thomas Firbank (and his agent, Linda Shaughnessy of A. P. Watt Ltd.) for permission to publish all these materials.

૭

Abbreviations of Principal References

Bio	Miriam J. Benkovitz. *Ronald Firbank: A Biography.* New York: Alfred A. Knopf, 1969.
Bib	Miriam J. Benkovitz. *A Bibliography of Ronald Firbank.* 2d ed. Oxford: Clarendon Press, 1982.
Brophy	Brigid Brophy. *Prancing Novelist: In Praise of Ronald Firbank.* London: Macmillan, 1973.
New Rythum	Ronald Firbank. *The New Rythum and Other Pieces.* Introduction by Alan Harris. London: Duckworth, 1962.
Swann	*Modern Literature: Sale Number 1421—Part II: The Miriam J. Benkovitz Collection.* New York: Swann Galleries, 1986. [Catalog for sale held 11 December 1986]

૭

True Love (3-11)

Text: typescript held by Rhees Library, University of Rochester. (*Bib* Ts 12.) Annotated "Not to publish R F" on title page. Excerpts published in *New Rythum* (119), otherwise previously unpublished.

Firbank began a "novel" called *Lila* at age ten (the surviving fragment is transcribed in *Bio,* 16-17), and a short story entitled "Mr. White-Morgan the Diamond King" at fourteen (Brophy 351 n. 4; extract in *New Rythum,* 115-16), but "True Love" appears to be his earliest completed "conte" (as he called his stories). Benkovitz guesses that Firbank composed it in 1903 while residing at Le Mortier de St. Symphorien, a suburb of Tours, where he was privately studying French (*Bio* 40-41). Firbank visited Spain at the end of 1902 (whence the Spanish details), and Brophy speculates (232) that Alwyn St. Claire takes his name from Rollo St. Clair Talboys, Firbank's instructor and mentor at Park Holm, a cramming establishment in Buxton, England.

When Widows Love (12-20)

Text: *"When Widows Love"* & *"A Tragedy in Green."* Edited by Edward Martin Potoker. London: Enitharmon Press, 1980, 17-24. (*Bib* A29.) Typescript annotated "Not to be published R F." Excerpts published (under the erroneous title "The Widow's Love") in *New Rythum* (116-17).

In September 1903 Firbank left St. Symphorien for Howley Grange near the village of St. Tulle in the Basses Alpes (to study French under M. A. Esclangon), where he probably wrote this story sometime that fall (*Bio* 42-43). Mrs. van Cotten, the American, reappears in Firbank's last, unfinished novel, *The New Rythum.*

A Study in Temperament (21-29)

Text: *"Odette D'Antrevernes" and "A Study in Temperament."*
London: Elkin Mathews, 1905, 31-45; Firbank's first book publication (*Bib* A1). Reprinted in *New Rythum* (19-29).

Firbank probably began this story at Howley Grange in the fall of 1903, for at the beginning of 1904 he sent a draft to Talboys for comment. Talboys supplied the title and made many other suggestions, most of which Firbank incorporated (*Bio* 43-44). Commenting on the characters' names, Brophy notes Firbank knew that Sevenoaks was Victoria Sackville-West's home (108) and that Lady Agnes's dressmaker Lucile was also Firbank's sister Heather's dressmaker (356).

There are about a dozen differences between the 1905 version of the story and the 1962 reprint in *New Rythum,* many of them improvements. However, since no explanation is given for these changes, and since nothing indicates Firbank ever revised this story (as he did "Odette" in the same volume: see Swann, lot 271), I've followed the 1905 version with these exceptions:

21.3] *siècle:* 1905 reads *siécle.*

24.3] Gordons': 1905 reads Gordon's.

24.28] Princess's: 1905 reads Princess'.

25.32] ideal: so reads the 1905; the 1962 version substitutes "idyll," which may make more sense, especially in light of Firbank's notoriously bad spelling. But since Firbank spelled phonetically (i.e., more likely to misspell "idyll" as "idle"), and since earlier on the same page Miss Tail attempts an epigram on "the ideal idol," I thought it safer to retain the earlier reading.

26.5] Saints!": 1905 reads Saints,"—changed in the 1962 version, as Brophy wryly notes, "presumably in the belief (which may, however, flatter Firbank) that the comma in the first edition is a misprint" (420 n.2). Even though there are numerous other run-on sentences in Firbank's early work, this one is particularly jarring, so I've adopted the exclamation point.

The *Times Literary Supplement* reviewed Firbank's first book in one sentence: "Two pieces—one a pretty old world story, and the other, less successful, of modern society" (9 June 1905, 187).

La Princesse aux Soleils (30-34)

Text: *"La Princesse aux Soleils"* & *"Harmonie."* Edited by Miriam J. Benkovitz. London: Enitharmon Press, 1974, 1-4. (*Bib* A27.) First published in *"Les Assais": Revue Mensuelle* 2 (November 1904): 78-80; Firbank's first periodical publication (*Bib* C1).

Firbank wrote this piece in April 1904, first in English, then translated it into French, and copied both versions into a pamphlet for his mother's birthday. (Firbank was living in Paris at the time, perfecting his French and cultivating his dandyism.) The pamphlet, with Firbank's own English version, was among the Firbank family's papers auctioned by Sotheby in 1961 (see the appendix to *New Rythum* for the sale catalog), and its whereabouts since then unknown. In her introduction to the Enitharmon edition, Benkovitz notes that in the pamphlet Firbank "added instructions for reciting the piece in French to Camille Saint-Saën's *Mélodies Persanes,* No. II 'La Splendeur vide' and No. V 'Au Cimitière.' "

Far Away (35-36)

Text: *"Far Away."* Edited by Miriam J. Benkovitz. [Iowa City:] University of Iowa, Typographic Laboratory, 1966. (*Bib* A22.)

Dated "Paris, 24th July 1904," this prose piece has been cataloged by some booksellers as poetry because of the short lines in the Iowa edition, transcribed exactly from the manuscript. (See Swann, lot 248, for a reproduction of the first page of the manuscript.) Benkovitz notes that Firbank had two versions of "Far Away" (*Bib* Ms 1 and Ts 2.1).

Odette d'Antrevernes (37-48)

Text: *"Odette D'Antrevernes" and "A Study in Temperament,"* 7-27. Firbank revised the text slightly when he reprinted it separately in 1916 (*Bib* A4), and this revised text is the version that appears in *The Works of Ronald Firbank* (1928; A12) and in *The Complete Ronald Firbank* (1961; A17). I've used the 1905 version because it is more consonant with the other texts in this volume; besides, as Brophy puts it, "he didn't and couldn't revise the twaddle out of it" (416). Although the title page of the 1905 edition capitalizes D'Antrevernes, the name appears as d'Antrevernes throughout the text and consequently I've adopted the lower case for the title as well.

"Odette" was written during the summer of 1904 and finished by September when Firbank returned to Paris after vacationing in the French Alps (*Bio* 51). Critics have said the style is from Maeterlinck and the content from Francis Jammes. Brophy offers an extended analysis of the tale (414-22).

Harmonie (49-51)

Text: *"La Princesse aux Soleils" & "Harmonie,"* 9-11. First published in *"Les Essais": Revue Mensuelle* 2 (February 1905): 305-6. (*Bib* C2.)

"La Princesse aux Soleils" was such a success with his mother that Firbank composed this piece for her for Christmas 1904. As Benkovitz explains in her introduction to the Enitharmon edition, it was copied into an "elaborate booklet entitled 'Ideas and Fancies.' It consisted of twenty pages with eight gold gauze interleaves, nine water-colours, and two compositions, ' "The Lieutenant & the Irise's Wife" a Parable' and 'Harmonie.' " (A page from *Ideas & Fancies* is reproduced in *New Rythum,* opposite p. 57; the parable was not considered for the present volume.)

The Legend of Saint Gabrielle (52-55)

Text: typescript in the hands of a private collector (*Bib* Ts 7). Annotated "Not to be published. RF" on title page; previously unpublished.

Benkovitz describes this as his next composition after "Harmonie," but states "Whether 'The Legend of St. Gabrielle' was written before Firbank left the Biais family in Paris [at the end of December 1904] or after is uncertain" (*Bio* 58). She also offers a psychological reading of the tale (*Bio* 56-57).

Souvenir d'Automne (56-57)

Text: *The King and His Navy and Army* 21 (2 December 1905): supplement, 11 (*Bib* C3).

The typescript, entitled "Impression d'Automne—A Poem in Prose," is dated 7 October 1905 and was written at The Coopers, the Firbank family home in Chislehurst (*Bio* 70). The published version is accompanied by an illustration: next page.

The Singing Bird & the Moon (58-65)

Text: typescript held by Rhees Library, University of Rochester. (*Bib* Ts 10.) Annotated "Not to be published RF" on title page; previously unpublished.

This and the following story date from the twelve-month period between October 1905 and September 1906; I've placed "The Singing Bird" first because it is, as Benkovitz says, "the last such effusion Firbank wrote" (*Bio* 71) before turning his full attention to society tales.

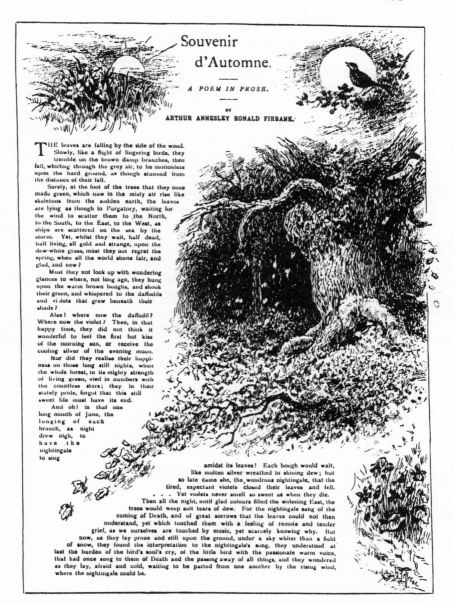

Souvenir d'Automne.

A POEM IN PROSE.

BY
ARTHUR ANNESLEY RONALD FIRBANK.

THE leaves are falling by the side of the wood. Slowly, like a flight of lingering birds, they tremble on the brown damp branches, then fall, whirling through the grey air, to lie motionless upon the hard ground, as though stunned from the distance of their fall.

Surely, at the foot of the trees that they once made green, which now in the misty air rise like skeletons from the sodden earth, the leaves are lying as though in Purgatory, waiting for the wind to scatter them to the North, to the South, to the East, to the West, as ships are scattered on the sea by the storm. Yet, whilst they wait, half dead, half living, all gold and strange, upon the dew-white grass, must they not regret the spring, when all the world shone fair, and glad, and new?

Must they not look up with wondering glances to where, not long ago, they hung upon the warm brown boughs, and shook their green, and whispered to the daffodils and violets that grew beneath their shade?

Alas! where now the daffodil? Where now the violet? Then, in that happy time, they did not think it wonderful to feel the first hot kiss of the morning sun, or receive the cooling silver of the evening moon.

Nor did they realise their happiness on those long still nights, when the whole forest, in its mighty strength of living green, vied in numbers with the countless stars; they in their stately pride, forgot that this still sweet life must have its end.

And oh! in that one long month of June, the longing of each branch, as night drew nigh, to have the nightingale to sing amidst its leaves! Each bough would wait, like molten silver wreathed in shining dew; but so late came she, the wondrous nightingale, that the tired, expectant violets closed their leaves and fell. . . . Yet violets never smell so sweet as when they die.

Then all the night, until glad colours filled the widening East, the trees would weep soft tears of dew. For the nightingale sang of the coming of Death, and of great sorrows that the leaves could not then understand, yet which touched them with a feeling of remote and tender grief, as we ourselves are touched by music, yet scarcely knowing why. But now, as they lay prone and still upon the ground, under a sky whiter than a field of snow, they found the interpretation to the nightingale's song, they understood at last the burden of the bird's soul's cry, of the little bird with the passionate warm voice, that had once sung to them of Death and the passing away of all things, and they wondered as they lay, afraid and cold, waiting to be parted from one another by the rising wind, where the nightingale could be.

Her Dearest Friend (66-73)

Text: typescript in the hands of a private collector (*Bib* Ts 3). Annotated "Not to be published" on title page; previously unpublished.

Benkovitz states this story was "composed either in December 1905 or January 1906," basing her conclusion on the reference (on p. 67 of this edition) to Strauss's *Salome,* which had its premiere on 9 December 1905 (*Bio* 71, 34 n.9). But as Brophy points out (313-15), this is a shaky foundation for assigning a date of composition, for the premiere was in Dresden, and *Salome* wouldn't premiere in London (where the story takes place) until 1910. It is possible, though Brophy says unlikely, that Firbank heard of the Dresden premiere and imagined it taking place in London, with Emma Calvé as the lead. (Calvé didn't sing in *Salome* at either premiere, though Firbank had known of her work for years, having written for her autograph in 1901 [*Bio* 28].) There are further complications: the story takes place on Lady Gouch's seventy-sixth birthday, and since she "seemed proud of being born in 1828" (66), that means the story occurs in 1904, at which time Strauss hadn't even finished *Salome.* The typescript lists his name as Arthur Firbank, a name he didn't use after 1907, so it would be unsafe to assign a date later than that. But what Benkovitz discerns as its undeveloped quality—as opposed to the more finished stories that follow—suggests 1906 as the most probable date of composition.

The Wavering Disciple (74-84)

Text: *Two Early Stories.* Edited by Miriam J. Benkovitz. New York: Albondocani Press, 1971, 13-27. (*Bib* A26.) First published in the *Granta* 20 (24 November 1906): 110-11 (parts I and II), and (5 December 1906): 130-32 (part III) (*Bib* C4-C5).

In her foreword to the Albondocani reprint, Benkovitz guesses Firbank "brought at least a part of 'The Wavering Disciple' with him when he came to Cambridge on 12 October 1906." It was apparently submitted first to Vyvyan Holland (Oscar Wilde's son) for the *Crescent,* the Trinity Hall magazine he edited; he rejected it, but it was accepted by another Cambridge undergraduate magazine, which published it in two installments. Like his heroine, Firbank was reading Thomas à Kempis that fall. "The Wavering Disciple" is among the works listed in the bibliographic chapter "The Misogynist's Library" in Alexander Theroux's novel *Darconville's Cat* (Garden City, NY: Doubleday, 1981), 445.

A Study in Opal (85-103)

Text: *Two Early Stories,* 31-54. First published in the *Granta* 21 (2 November 1907): 54-60 (*Bib* C6).

In her foreword Benkovitz states "the composition of 'A Study in Opal' . . . went on during a visit to Bermuda and Jamaica in June and July and one to Belgium in September 1907." As she also points out, Lady Henrietta Worthing's desire for her own stained-glass window anticipates the story line of Firbank's first full-length novel, *Vainglory* (1915). And as Brophy points out (282), the name Worthing is Wildean in inspiration—as is so much in early Firbank.

A Tragedy in Green (104-16)

Text: *"When Widows Love"* & *"A Tragedy in Green,"* 26-36. Typescript annotated "Not to be published RF" (*Bib* Ts 11). Excerpts published in *New Rythum* (118-19).

"Composed in 1907 or 1908," writes Benkovitz, who notes that the heroine, Lady Georgia Blueharnis, also appears in *Vainglory.* There is a Lord Blueharnis as well as a Lady Seafairer (perhaps the Jane Seafairer on Lady Georgia's "hit list" [109]) in Firbank's unpublished one-act play *A Disciple from the Country,* apparently written a year or so after "A Tragedy in Green" (excerpt in *New Rythum,* 120-26). The dedicatee, Sir Coleridge Kennard, was a friend of Firbank's during his Cambridge days (1906–9) and later wrote the introduction to Firbank's post-humous novel *The Artificial Princess* (1934). (That introduction, by the way, is reprinted with numerous other essays on Firbank in Mervyn Horder's excellent anthology *Ronald Firbank: Memoirs and Critiques* [London: Duckworth, 1977].)

Lady Appledore's Mésalliance (117-49)

Text: *New Rythum,* 33-67; appeared simultaneously in *Cornhill Magazine* 172 (Summer 1962): 399-425 (*Bib* A19, C9). Annotated "? Revise considerably in places—If—" (*Bib* Ts 6). It doesn't appear the editor of *New Rythum* regularized this text as he did "A Study in Temperament," but the original manuscript (sold at the Swann sale of Benkovitz's library) was not available for comparison. Names of flowers are capitalized throughout, no doubt in deference to the pastoral mode, and have been retained here (along with some inconsistencies that only Firbank could explain).

Written "probably in 1907 or 1908," Brophy argues that "In the concentrated metaphor of the story, Firbank was probably recording his expulsion (in 1907) from the paradise-garden of The Coopers, Chislehurst, and its emotional consequence, his reception (in December 1907) into the Catholic church at the hands of Hugh Benson. At the same time, Firbank was making, by the artificiality of his pastoral, a retort by satire to the back-to-nature message of Benson's novel *The Sentimentalists*" (334). Benkovitz notes that at a 1905 dinner party in Madrid "Firbank confided his resolution that 'should he ever be obliged to earn his living he would become a gardener,' a circumstance later chron-icled in 'Lady Appledore's Mésalliance' " (*Bio* 63-64). Like other early Firbank heroines, Lady Appledore is mentioned in *Vain-glory.*

Appendix (151-55)

The poem "The Wind & the Roses" and the essay "An Early Flemish Painter" are included here because they date from the same period as the stories and thus round out this record of Firbank's literary development.

The text of the poem is from *"The Wind & the Roses,"* edited by Miriam J. Benkovitz (London: privately printed for Alan Clodd, 1965). (*Bib* A21.) In her introduction, Benkovitz states "it can not be dated more exactly than at some time before Christmas 1904," but in her biography says it could have been written as early as 1902 (*Bio* 34). She prints an exact transcript of Firbank's manuscript, grammatical warts and all. For this edition, errors have been corrected. A revised version of the first stanza appears in chapter 9 of *Vainglory,* where it is said to be from Miss Hospice's *Scroll from the Fingers of Ta-Hor,* "in which, steeping herself in deception and mystery, she attempts to out-Chatterton Chatterton."

"An Early Flemish Painter" is reprinted from a pamphlet of the same name, privately printed in 1969 as a Christmas greeting "for the friends of the Enitharmon Press and Miriam J. Benkovitz" (*Bib* A24). First published in the *Academy* 73 (28 September 1907): 948 (*Bib* C5.1, where the date is incorrectly given as 1903). Firbank visited Bruges at the end of August 1907, where he saw six portraits of Emperor Charles V at the Exposition. He wrote the essay the following month and submitted it to his friend Alfred Douglas, the new editor of the *Academy.* In her introductory note (from which the foregoing has been adapted), Benkovitz notes that Firbank seems to have confused details from several portraits of Charles V, but no matter: the essay is of interest chiefly as an extension of his prose-poem experiments (compare "Far Away") and for Firbank's obvious empathy with the Flemish painter and parallel development. Like Gossart, Firbank began with imitations of received styles, and then, after immersion in Continental life and literature, "his work becomes an experiment. . . . He begins to drape his figures in the Italian style, making use lavishly of pearls and precious stones, of flowers, and birds of brilliant plumage, and amidst this splendour he sets anxious-looking Flemish Madonnas, a little bewildered, perhaps, at this new luxury. . . . The effect is curious."

STEVEN MOORE